FORBIDDEN

CLAUDE

❧

ELIZABETH ROSE

Patricia,
Enjoy the adventure!
Elizabeth Rose

ROSESCRIBE MEDIA INC.

Copyright © 2018 by Elizabeth Rose Krejcik

This is a work of fiction. All characters, names, places, and incidents are either a product of the author's imagination or used fictitiously. Any similarity to actual organizations or persons living or deceased is entirely coincidental. All rights reserved. No part of this book may be used, reproduced or transmitted in any form whatsoever without the author's written permission.

Cover created by Elizabeth Rose Krejcik
Edited by Scott Moreland

ISBN-13: 978-1987550283
ISBN-10: 1987550285

TO MY READERS

This book is the story of the son of my hero and heroine, John Montague and Celestine de Bar from *The Baron's Destiny – Book 3* of my *Barons of the Cinque Ports Series.*

It is a standalone book, but it is better to read The Baron's Destiny first so no surprises will be ruined.

I had an overwhelming request for Claude's story from my readers. If you've already read *The Baron's Destiny*, you will realize Claude is in love with a girl named Rose – daughter of one of the other barons, but she is in love with someone else. So now, Claude will finally get his chance at happily-ever-after, as long as he can stop carrying the torch for Rose.

In this story, you will be introduced to the other Barons of the Cinque Ports from the rest of the series:

Lord Nicholas Vaughn & wife Muriel – *The Baron's Quest – Book 1*
Lord Conlin de Braose & wife Isobel – *The Baron's Bounty – Book 2*
Lord John Montague & wife Celestine (Claude's parents) - *The Baron's Destiny – Book 3*

At the end of the book you will find a list of not only the barons and their wives but also their children that they had after their stories ended.

Thank you, and enjoy,

Elizabeth Rose

CHAPTER 1

Second in Command

PORT OF SANDWICH, ENGLAND 1294

*C*laude Jean Montague returned to England only to have his heart broken once again.

Love hurt. Claude learned this at the young age of five and ten years when he had his heart broken the first time by Lady Rose of Sandwich. Daughter of Baron Conlin de Braose of the Cinque Ports, Rose had shown kindness to Claude when he and his mother first arrived in Hastings from France, eight years ago. It had been during a trying time in Claude's life because that was when he first met his father. He had hoped to one day marry the girl, but she had eyes for her father's squire, Toft, instead.

Had Claude known he was about to walk right back into the hardships of the past and that it would bring all those old feelings rising to the surface again, he never would have agreed to make the trip to England to celebrate his younger sister's birthday.

Having sailed to Sandwich from France where he'd been living for the past six years, Claude had plenty of time to think about the girl he once loved. But Rose was married to someone else now, he reminded himself. She wouldn't feel the same way about him that he felt for her. This fact was hard to accept.

"Mon Seigneur, nous approchons les quais de Sandwich," Claude's squire so generously pointed out they had approached the docks. Claude didn't speak his native language much anymore. Even though he'd returned to his homeland of France when he inherited his late grandfather's castle and demesne, he felt like more of an Englishman than French after finding out that Baron John Montague of Hastings was his father.

"Oui," Claude answered. "Felix, it would be better if we spoke in English while we are on English soil," he pointed out. "My father is not fond of the French language."

"Aye, my lord," said Felix.

Claude's eyes fixated on Briarbeck Castle in the distance as the ship sailed into the harbor. Rose would be there with her husband, Toft. His heart sped up. He longed to see her but dreaded it at the same time. Confusion welled within him. The flame of love still burned in his heart for Lady Rose, inhibiting him to take a wife even though he was already three and twenty years of age. Rose didn't see him in the same light. She considered them naught but friends. Her love was only for her husband, Toft.

The ship docked, and Claude made his way to the boarding plank to disembark.

"The docks are crowded today, my lord," said his squire, carrying Claude's travel bag over his shoulder as they headed down the pier. Sandwich was a major port of trade and one of the Cinque Ports along with New Romney, Dover, Hastings, and Hythe. Claude's father was the Baron of the Cinque Ports of Hastings, but he resided in Winchelsea now that Hastings was too silted up for ships to dock. A storm eight years ago ruined the harbor, and took many lives as well as dumped half of Castle Hastings into the sea. His father had a hard time coming to terms with the fact he had lost his prestigious castle to an act of God.

Heartbreak was no stranger to Claude's family. Claude's sad and lonesome childhood and his mother's stories of watching her mother burn at the stake were things that haunted him yet. He wished he could forget them forever.

"Do you see your mother?" asked Felix, stepping around two dockworkers hauling a trunk from a nearby ship. Fishermen carried poles and bait buckets, loading them onto their small vessels that bobbed up and down in the waves. Ships of all sizes filled the harbor, flying the flags of nobles and even foreign lords that arrived there for trade.

The slips closest to the dock held the smaller fishing vessels and flat-bottomed cogs that could sail right up to the docks to unload. The larger trade ships that needed deeper water so as not to be marooned, anchored further out and the occupants took shuttle boats to the pier.

"Nay, I don't see her," said Claude, scanning the pier and the many people that ranged from sailors, fishermen, and nobles, to dockworkers and even beggars. A baker carrying a tray over his head sold loaves of brown bread. An old alewife followed in his steps with her husband, pushing a cart with buckets of ale, a ladle, and some wooden cups. A lame man sat on the edge of the pier begging, talking with a fishmonger who kept busy shucking a bucket of oysters.

The sounds and smells of the sea and the salty summer breeze filled Claude's nostrils bringing back memories of the first time he visited England. He was a skinny, insecure, and angry boy back then. He had changed much in the past eight years, and his father was to thank. John Montague took Claude as his squire and trained him for two years before Claude decided he could no longer stay in England. He'd continued his training in France with his mentors and advisors while ruling over his new demesne at Stonebury Castle.

Claude was a knight now, not just a scared boy. Would Rose notice? And would she even care?

In the distance, he saw his father's ship, *The Poseidon*, docked next to Lord Conlin's ship, *Lady Bellacose*. Lord Nicholas Vaughn's ship, *The WindStorm*, was there as well. His father was a good friend to the other Barons of the Cinque Ports, being very close with Lord Conlin de Braose of Sandwich and Lord Nicholas Vaughn of New Romney. Claude missed these men as well as their families. They had been kind to him and his mother and accepted them with open arms. He felt an ache in his chest and wondered now if he'd been wrong in staying away so long.

"Father's ship is docked, so my family must be here already," Claude told Felix.

"Did you ever discover why your parents wanted you to come to Sandwich instead of meeting with them in Winchelsea?" asked the squire.

"Nay. The missive didn't say, although I suppose it has something to do with my sister Charlotte's birthday. My father is a close friend of Baron Sandwich as well as Baron Romney. Perhaps they are throwing a celebration here because Briarbeck Castle has the most space."

"Claude, Claude!" shouted a woman from the crowd.

Claude turned his head to see his mother waving her hand over her head. It had been nearly six months now since his mother last visited him in France with Claude's sister, Charlotte, and his Uncle Lucio. Since Claude refused to return to England, his mother came back to France to visit at least twice a year.

Claude's father, John, stood next to her with little Charlotte perched like a bird on his shoulders.

"Brother," he heard Charlotte call out, clapping her hands and smiling. The little girl was so excited to see him that she tried to stand up and almost fell.

"John, put Charlotte down. That is no way to treat a young lady," said Claude's mother, Celestine.

Claude smiled as he approached them. He missed this type of banter since his isolated life without a father had been very quiet, indeed.

"Charlotte is going to get hurt," Celestine continued.

"Wife, you worry too much," grumbled Claude's father, leaning over and giving his wife a peck on the cheek. "Besides, Charlotte wanted to watch for Claude."

"You tend to forget she is not a boy!"

"Mother," said Claude, hurrying to embrace his mother in a hug. He kissed her on each cheek.

"*Claude, mon fils. Tu es un bon chevalier,*" said his mother, reverting to their native tongue, telling him he was a fine knight. "*Ça fait trop longtemps que je t'ai vu.*"

"*Je tu ai vu il y a moins d'un an. Ma mère, ne pleure pas!*" Claude assured his mother it had been less than a year since they'd last parted and that she should not cry.

"My lord," said Felix, clearing his throat. The squire's eyes darted over to John who was scowling at them. Felix leaned in and spoke in a low voice. "I thought you said not to speak French since your father doesn't like it."

"That's right," said John, overhearing him. He took Charlotte off his shoulders and gently lowered her to the ground. "You two are not in France anymore. Speak English when you are on English soil."

"Haven't you learned the language by now, Father?" asked Claude with a smile. "Or is it too hard for you?" he teased.

"I have tried to teach him, but he is as stubborn as an old goat," complained Celestine, putting her hands on her hips. "Every other noble in the country can speak French. But your father has it set in his mind that he doesn't need to know it."

"Every other noble has wasted valuable time that could have been used in learning fighting skills instead." John stepped forward and extended his arm. "Claude, I've missed you, Son." He pulled Claude to him and gave his son a manly slap on the back. "I almost didn't recognize you. You've grown into a man. You have muscles that weren't there last time I saw you." He stepped back and perused Claude with a proud smile. Then he swatted at Claude's head. "I am glad you no longer have that long hair in your eyes like a girl."

It had been nearly three years since Claude had seen his father. Claude and John had been inseparable when John first found out he had a son. He pushed hard to make up for the fifteen years he'd missed in Claude's life. Claude enjoyed the attention at first, but then he started feeling smothered. He also had an extremely hard time being around Rose and not being able to have her as his own. He'd left England, upsetting his father who took it as a personal blow after all the hardships he'd been through. John eventually forgave Claude for leaving but had only visited him a few times in France in the past six years.

"If you had visited our son in France more often, it wouldn't be this way," Celestine reminded her husband.

"Celestine, you know I have been busy with handling the new port of Winchelsea, as well as overseeing the construction of my new castle. Besides, Claude could have visited me here, yet he didn't. And you know I don't like to go to France unless I'm sent there by the king."

"Why not, Father?" asked little Charlotte, looking up with big blue eyes.

"Because your father almost died there," Celestine told her, reaching down to pull her daughter closer.

John rubbed his shoulder that had at one time been shot with an arrow right before he was thrown from his horse and was left dangling off the edge of a cliff in France.

"Who tried to kill him?" asked Charlotte in a squeaky little voice filled with concern.

John faked a cough, shaking his head, warning Celestine not to tell the child that Celestine had been the one to almost do him in.

"Charlotte, come here," said Claude, bending over and holding out his arms. Charlotte ran to him and he scooped her up, holding her in one arm as he tickled her with the other. Claude had been fifteen years old when his sister was born. He had lived most of his life as an only child. Charlotte laughed and pushed Claude's hand away and then reached out and mussed his hair.

"She's a real feisty one, isn't she?" asked Felix with a chuckle.

"She gets that from her mother," said John. Celestine playfully hit John on the shoulder. He slipped his arm around her waist and turned and headed for the horses. "Let's get back to the castle for the celebration."

Claude was surprised by the crowd on the docks today. There were also plenty of ships in the harbor. He put Charlotte on the ground and held her hand as they walked. "Is there a trade fair going on?" he asked his father.

"Nay, why do you ask?" John answered over his shoulder.

"I can't believe how crowded it is on the port of Sandwich today."

"They're here for the celebration," John told him, helping Celestine to mount a horse and then mounting one as well. "Claude, we brought a horse for you. Charlotte can ride back to the castle with you, but your squire will have to walk."

"Felix, meet us at the castle," said Claude, lifting his sister up into the saddle.

"Aye, my lord," said Felix with a nod. "I will make certain your things are transferred to the castle from the ship."

Claude pulled himself up behind Charlotte. "My, Charlotte, I had no idea you were so important that all these people are coming to celebrate your birthday."

"I'm going to be eight," Charlotte announced.

"Yes, I know," said Claude, turning the horse.

"Claude, wait." His mother rode to his side. "I think you have the wrong impression why I've called you to Sandwich."

"The missive said you wanted me here to participate in the celebration and that Charlotte was looking forward to it. I figured you were talking about her birthday."

"I did say that, but it wasn't just Charlotte's birthday I meant."

"It wasn't?" Claude chuckled. "Well, I know it's not your birthday, and neither is it Father's, so what do you mean? I don't make a journey to England for anyone unless they are important to me."

"That's right," said John. "That is why your mother sent for you even though I told her it was a bad idea."

"What was a bad idea?" asked Claude, feeling a knot forming in his stomach. Somehow, he knew he wasn't going to like the answer. "What is it we are celebrating?"

"Hello, Claude," came a voice from a horse and cart that pulled up next to him. Claude slowed his horse and turned around. His eyes fell on Lady Rose sitting inside the cart next to another woman who was driving.

"Rose." His voice came out barely above a whisper. Instantly, he became tongue-tied and didn't know what to say. His heart sped up, and the pounding of his pulse in his ears grew deafening.

Here was Rose, no longer a young girl like when he'd left her. Instead, she was a curvy, beautiful woman. Her long, blond hair was pulled back in a braid, and her bright blue eyes twinkled in the sunlight as she smiled at him. Dressed in a burgundy velvet gown, she looked like a princess with the metal, jeweled circlet on her head.

"It is such a surprise to see you," she told him, sounding very pleased. Her voice was soft and sweet, just how he'd remembered. "This is my nursemaid, Evelina," she said, nodding toward the woman next to her, but Claude wasn't looking at anyone but Rose.

Finally, Claude found the words to speak. "My mother

sent me a message to come to England. She told me she would not take no for answer. I am here for the birthday celebration," he told her.

"I didn't think you'd come since you never even sent a missive when my brothers Dunmor and Harry were born."

A little boy popped his head up over the back of the wagon seat. Big, brown eyes stared at him in question.

"I'll bet you're Harry," said Claude. "Where are your brothers?" Claude only knew one of Rose's brothers. When he trained as his father's squire for two years, Rose's brother, Torrence, had been born to her father and his new Scottish wife, Isobel.

"Yes, this is Harry, but he is shy and doesn't talk to strangers," Rose explained. "Today is his birthday, and he is four years old."

It didn't feel right to Claude when Rose referred to him as a stranger, but he realized that was precisely what he was. He had left when Rose married Toft, never having the courage to return. It had been too hard to watch Rose being in love with Toft when all he ever wanted was for her to be in love with him.

"So, it looks as if there is a double birthday celebration after all," said Claude, holding tighter to his sister as she squirmed and almost fell out of the saddle.

"Aye, my parents are back at the castle preparing for the feast," Rose informed him. "They will be happy to see you after all this time. Toft is there, too. My husband will be anxious to see you again as well. We are all happy you finally came back to England."

Rose referring to Toft as her husband was like a knife being plunged directly into Claude's heart. He had no desire to see Toft, although he held nothing against the man. Nothing that is, except for the fact that he married the girl that Claude wanted for his own.

"My lady," said the nursemaid, Evelina, speaking ever so softly. She seemed to be hiding her face under the hood of her cape, and all Claude could see were shadows. "You shouldn't be out here on the docks. Your husband will not be happy that you left the castle in your condition."

"Neither will your father be happy, Rose," added John, turning and riding his horse back to join them. "You know how protective Conlin is about things like this."

"Things like what?" asked Claude, feeling shaken since it was apparent there was something they were all hiding from him.

Rose smiled at Claude and rubbed her belly. "This is what they are talking about, Claude. I was the one who asked Celestine to summon you. But it wasn't because of Harry or Charlotte's birthdays. It was because I have been ill lately. My father and husband are leaving tomorrow to give their two weeks' service to the king. I was frightened and wanted you here in their absence when I birthed my baby."

Claude's eyes focused on the large swell of Rose's stomach. She looked as if she were going to pop. He'd been so entranced by her eyes he hadn't even noticed her belly until now. "Y-you're pregnant," he stammered.

"Yes, I am. And after losing two babies in the past six

years, my father is very worried I will lose this one, too. You remember that he has lost five children as well as a wife. Although he has three sons now with Isobel, I am his only daughter. I want more than anything to give him grandchildren, but I have to admit I am terrified that it might never happen."

Claude was surprised at hearing Rose had lost two babies and didn't know what to say. "Nay, don't be frightened," said Claude, instantly wanting to comfort the girl the way she'd comforted him so many years ago.

"I won't be frightened anymore now that you are here, Claude," she told him. "You are a good friend of mine. It broke my heart when you left England and didn't return."

If only she knew he'd left because she had broken his heart in more ways than one.

"My lady, please," begged Evelina, very anxious to leave. "We need to get back to the castle, *tout de suite*."

Claude's head snapped up at hearing the nursemaid speak French. She sounded different than an Englishwoman speaking his language. He heard something in her voice that told him she was from his homeland.

"Are you from France?" he asked the girl. Her body stiffened, and she grabbed the reins of the horse tighter. She didn't answer, and neither did she look at him.

"Evelina is right, we shouldn't be here," said Rose. "I was so excited to see you that we didn't even wait for an escort. I wanted to meet you on the docks when you disembarked and had Evelina drive the cart. You look so different. You are . . . a man now, Claude."

Rose smiled at him and then nodded to her nursemaid to take them back to the castle. They sped away over the wharf leaving Claude staring after them, not knowing what to think.

"I am sorry I didn't tell you, Claude," said his mother softly. "Rose asked me not to. She thought if you knew she was pregnant, you wouldn't come."

That was the truth. Claude wouldn't have set foot on English soil if he'd known Rose was pregnant. He also hadn't heard until now that she'd lost two children before this. Then again, it was probably his fault since he purposely never asked about her, wanting to forget her. He had told his mother to never mention Rose's name, and so she had respected his wishes and never said a thing.

"Are you going to go back to France now, Claude?" Charlotte looked up at him with sad eyes.

How could he leave her? He had to be there for his sister. Not to mention, now he felt as if he needed to be here for Rose as well. He couldn't let either of them down. It was his duty as a knight, a brother, and a friend. Anger gripped his gut, but he held back the emotions threatening to spill forth. "Nay, of course not. I won't leave, Charlotte," he said, kissing his little sister atop her head. "I came for a birthday celebration, and that is what you are going to get. Just wait until you see the present I brought you."

"A present? For me?" Her eyes lit up with excitement. "Oh, Claude, give it to me now."

Claude chuckled. "Nay, my sweet, little sister. You are

going to have to wait until the feast. I will not give you your present a minute sooner."

"Then hurry, Claude. Ride fast to the castle. I can't wait to get there," Charlotte urged him.

John turned and led the way, but Celestine stared at Claude with pity in her eyes.

"I'm sorry, Claude," she whispered as he rode past.

"Me too," said Claude, holding tightly to Charlotte as he dug his heels into the sides of the horse and directed the animal into a run. He felt like a man heading to the gallows. Going back to the castle where he would have to watch Rose with her husband was the last thing he wanted to do right now. But Rose was counting on him. She was frightened. How could he leave her when she had been there for him in his time of need?

CHAPTER 2

Second in Command

"Evelina, slow down," exclaimed Rose as Evelina drove the cart much too fast for having a child and a pregnant lady aboard.

"I'm sorry, my lady." Evelina slowed the cart as they headed for the castle.

"You are acting very uptight ever since we came to the docks," said Rose. "What is the matter?"

Evelina had kept hidden when she saw the ship from France. At first, she had thought her father was aboard it, or perhaps her betrothed. She didn't want to marry the wretched Lord Onfroi Faucheux of Grenoble. That is why she left France in the first place. She realized alliances were necessary, but she was not willing to offer herself up as a sacrificial lamb. Nay, she would not marry the evil man because if she did, her life would be over. He was old and cruel and liked to beat women. She'd even heard from the kitchen maids that Lord Onfroi had tied up some of the servant girls from his castle and forced himself on them.

Her father didn't believe her, and there was nothing she could do to convince him it was true. So, she did the only thing she could to keep her from this doomed fate. She stowed away on a ship to England wearing the clothes of a peasant. Accompanied by no one but Augustin, one of her father's mercenaries, she was lucky enough to meet the kind-hearted Lady Rose on the docks who had taken her in as a nursemaid.

Of course, Evelina had forged a letter of recommendation, being skilled in faking signatures and handwriting of any kind. To get Augustin to be her escort, she had to pay him dearly. Their story was that he was her brother, even though he was a good fifteen years older than her. He was hired as a guard at Briarbeck Castle so they could stay together. Evelina's real surname was du Pont, but she was using the alias of Bisset.

For a fortnight now, Evelina lived in disguise, giving up her life as a noble in hopes of finding an Englishman with whom she could fall in love and marry. If anyone discovered her true identity, she would be sent back to France immediately and be married off to Lord Onfroi in a heartbeat.

"Naught is wrong, Lady Rose. I just don't think it is safe for you to be on the docks, that's all."

"We were in no danger with Lord John and Sir Claude there," Rose assured her. "Now that Claude will be here in my father and husband's absence, I am not even afraid to give birth."

"He'll be here that long?" Evelina didn't like the fact Sir Claude was from France and wasn't leaving anytime soon. Plus, she'd made a mistake when she spoke, and he was now aware she was French as well. If he stayed at Briarbeck Castle, there was no doubt he would be asking questions that she didn't want to answer. She didn't know him, but what if he knew of her?

"I am sorry, my lady. I spoke out of line." Evelina played the subservient position of a servant even though she was the daughter of a French count. She enjoyed being around children, and Rose was a kind person. Still, it was hard having to remember that she now had to sit below the salt and eat with the commoners. She couldn't wear velvet or jewels anymore and had to sleep on a pallet on the floor in Lady Rose's wardrobe.

As awful as this all was, the one good thing was that she could come and go without being noticed. She could also observe the eligible Englishmen and would, hopefully, find one who took her interest. She planned on finding a man to marry here in England. Then she would send a missive back to France and, hopefully, convince her father to change her betrothal.

Being in England gave her the opportunity to do this, although it was probably a risky and foolish thing to do. However, if she had stayed in France, everyone knew her and she would never be able to hide in the shadows like she was doing here. It was her last chance to make her life the way she wanted it to be. Her two brothers were already married. Being the youngest and only daughter, her father had plans for her that she didn't agree with and never would.

"I have known Claude for a long time," said Rose as Evelina brought the cart to a stop. "We are good friends. Did you know he wanted to marry me at one time, but I turned him down?"

"He did?" Evelina handed the reins to a stable boy as she slipped off the driver's seat. "He is very handsome, my lady. Why would you turn him down?" She held out her arms for Harry, lifting him from the cart and holding his hand.

Rose walked around the cart, coming to Evelina's side. "I had just turned three and ten years of age at the time. I was in love with my father's squire, Toft. That is why I married him instead of Claude. My father agreed because he wanted me to be happy, even though Toft was not from a rich family and didn't own an estate. Oh, here is my husband now."

Evelina stepped to the side as Toft rushed over to greet his wife. He hugged her and kissed her in front of everyone, scooping her up into his arms. That made Rose giggle.

"Pick me up, too," said Harry, holding out his arms.

"Toft, put me down," scolded Rose. "If you don't, I might deliver this baby right in your arms."

"I wish you would," said Toft. His bright eyes sparkled in the sun, and his honey-colored hair gently lifted in the warm breeze. "If you did that, I wouldn't have to worry about you every minute I am away." He placed Rose on her feet.

Evelina's heart melted, watching the couple that looked to be so much in love. That's what she wanted, too. She wanted a man to fall in love with her. Someday, she hoped to have a kind and handsome young husband who would kiss and hug her and care about having a child so much that he didn't want to leave her. Yes, she wanted someone just like Toft.

"You don't have to worry about me being alone when I birth the baby, Toft," Rose told her husband.

Toft looked over to Evelina. "Aye, I know you have the nursemaid."

"And me," said Harry. "I will help my sister."

"I'm sure you will," said Toft, ruffling the little boy's hair. "Your mother will be here, too, but I don't feel as if that is enough."

"Sir Toft, I heard what ye said." Isobel, Rose's Scottish stepmother, approached holding on to the arm of Rose's father, Lord Conlin de Braose. Isobel was once sent as a proxy from Scotland but ended up falling in love with Conlin, and they were married instead. "I assure ye I will take guid care of my daughter and her bairn. Ye have nothin' to worry about."

Conlin spoke up next. "The only thing you have to fear is if my wife will have the baby's feet in shoes by the time we return," Conlin said with a chuckle.

"I don't understand," said Evelina.

"My father is jesting." Rose threw a sideways glance at her father.

"Like hell I am," mumbled Conlin. "We have all seen Isobel's crazy infatuation with shoes, and there is no telling what is going to happen next where that is concerned."

"Conlin, ye are exaggeratin'," said Isobel. "I havena even bought a new pair of shoes for some time now."

"Really?" he asked, glancing across the courtyard. "Torrence, Dunmor, come here," he called out to their eight and six-year-old sons who came running.

"What is it, Father?" asked Dunmor.

"You aren't leaving yet, are you?" Torrence inquired.

"Nay, boys. I won't be leaving until the morrow. Harry, come here, too, please."

Harry ran over, and Conlin scooped him up in his arms.

"Conlin, what is this all about?" asked Isobel.

"Show me your shoes, boys," said Conlin.

"Our shoes?" asked Torrence, confused.

"That's right," said Conlin, holding up one of Harry's feet. The little boy giggled. "Let me see your shoes."

Torrence and Dunmor held one foot in the air, showing off brand new boots.

"Uh huh," said Conlin with a nod.

"Conlin, what are ye doin'?" asked Isobel.

"Boys, you were wearing shoes, not boots this morning, weren't you?"

"Yes, Father," said Torrence.

"So, why did you change them?"

ELIZABETH ROSE

"Mother bought us new boots, and she wanted to see how they fit," Dunmor blurted out.

Evelina had to hold back her laughter when she saw Isobel's face redden at the tattling of her son.

"Isobel?" asked Conlin in a low voice. "What do you have to say about that?"

"Oh, all right, so I bought the bairns some new shoes. But I didna buy any for myself."

"Good thing," said Conlin, placing Harry on the ground. "Any more shoes and I will have to add a room to the castle just to store them all. Now, come on, boys, we need to get to the great hall for someone's birthday celebration."

"Me? Do you mean me?" asked Harry, sounding so excited that Evelina thought he would wet himself.

"Yes, you," said Conlin. "We have a celebration! Now, everyone get to the great hall so we can start."

"Did you want me to watch over the children?" Evelina asked Conlin.

"Nay, not tonight. I'll watch the boys. You stay close to my daughter, instead," Conlin called back over his shoulder. "If she shows any signs of starting to birth the baby, report to me or my wife immediately, do you understand?"

"Aye, my lord," said Evelina with a nod.

"Rose, I don't think I should leave tomorrow," Toft told his wife. "You might need me."

"Thank you, Husband, but you don't have a choice. It is your duty as a knight to serve the king when needed. And as I was saying, I will be in good hands. Claude is here. Here he comes now."

"Claude de Bar is here from France?" Toft looked up to see Claude dismounting his horse. "Claude. Over here," shouted Toft, waving his hand in the air.

"Remember, he is Claude Montague now since his father has claimed him," Rose told her husband. "Sir Claude. He is a knight as well."

"Aye, that's right." Toft chuckled lowly. "I can't help but wonder how that scrawny little boy with the long hair in his eyes managed to become a knight."

"He doesn't look like that anymore, Toft, so please be nice."

Evelina saw the handsome Frenchman looking in their direction. He helped his young sister from the horse and sent her over to his parents before he headed over. Evelina kept her eyes downward, not wanting the man to see her face.

"Hello, Toft," said Claude, reaching out and clasping hands with Rose's husband.

"My, you have grown up since the last time I saw you, Claude. I'm surprised to see you here," Toft replied. "After all, you left so suddenly after Rose and I married that I didn't even get to say farewell."

"It's been six years since Claude went back to France," said Rose. "But he is here now and is going to watch over me until your return, so you needn't worry. I will be in good hands."

"You are going to do that?" Toft seemed pleased.

Evelina glanced up to see Claude and Rose's eyes interlock. Rose was smiling, but Claude wasn't. The man held discomfort in his gaze. She could tell he was uptight by the rigidness of his stance.

"Well, I am not sure how long I'll be able to stay," Claude muttered, fidgeting as he answered.

"Rose is due to have our baby any day now." Toft pulled Rose closer, giving his wife a squeeze. "You won't have long to wait. I assure you of that."

Evelina witnessed the uneasiness in Claude's eyes before he looked down to his arm, pretending to brush away lint. The happy couple didn't even seem to notice that Claude felt uncomfortable. Evelina wondered if it had something to do with the fact Claude once wanted to marry Rose. Perhaps, he still had feelings for her after all this time.

"Claude, you will be here for me until Toft returns, won't you?" Rose asked with hope in her voice.

"My service to the king is for a fortnight. I will return as soon as I can," Toft informed him. "I would feel at ease knowing Rose has a man she can trust at her side. I don't want her to feel afraid . . . after losing the last two babies and all."

CLAUDE WAS at a loss for words. How could he not stay when Rose wanted him there? Even though Rose had already explained things, now that Toft had also pointed out she'd lost two babies, he realized she was frightened and rightly so. Guilt ate away at him for not even expressing his sorrow for their loss.

"Of course, I'd be happy to stay at Rose's side until your return," agreed Claude. "I also want to offer my condolences on the hardships you two have experienced in the past years. I am sorry, but I didn't know about the loss of your babies until today."

"You didn't know?" asked Toft. His brows dipped in confusion.

"Didn't your mother tell you?" asked Rose. "After all, she visits you in France several times a year."

"Nay, she didn't mention it." Claude felt like a heel and cursed himself inwardly for burying his head in the sand. He had to explain things, or his mother would look like the fool. "I asked her not to tell me any bad news, so it isn't her fault. I was going through . . . some rough times. I am sorry."

Rose reached out and touched Claude lightly on the shoulder. His body stiffened and he held his breath, not wanting to feel the warmth of her hand on him. It was just too much to bear.

"I understand, Claude," said Rose. "It's all right."

There was an awkward silence between them. Claude felt the heat rising to his face. He had to say something and didn't want to talk about Rose, her baby or Toft anymore. It was just too hard to take. He turned and looked at the nursemaid instead. She stood there so quietly that he had almost forgotten she was there. Her face was turned to the ground.

"I'm sorry, Nursemaid, but what was your name again?"

he asked, knowing it was Evelina, but wanting the girl to speak so he would have someone else to talk to.

The girl's eyes snapped up in surprise, and he got his first look at her face. A round face with big, hazel eyes stared up at him almost as if in fear. She was a petite girl, with a small frame. Her oaken hair was braided and coiled around each ear and covered partially by a wimple. It reminded him of the way the nobles wore their hair. Her skin was fair and smooth. She seemed to be a few years younger than his age of twenty-three.

"*Moi?*" she asked in surprise, then corrected herself quickly. "Me?" Her eyes shot back to the ground.

"Her name is Evelina," Rose told him.

"Evelina," he repeated, thinking it was the prettiest name he'd ever heard. The prettiest name, that is, besides Rose. "Does she have a surname?" he asked.

"She does," said Rose. "But perhaps you should ask her directly."

Claude reached out and lifted the girl's chin with two fingers. Her face turned upward, but her eyes would not meet his.

"Look at me," he said, wanting to get another glimpse of her magnificent, large eyes.

EVELINA HAD no choice but to look into Sir Claude's eyes. If she didn't, she would be disobeying orders to a noble. She wondered if this is how all servants felt. It wasn't a good feeling at all.

"That's better," he said, studying her face, cocking his dark head to each side as he inspected her as if she were a side of beef. His eyes were bright blue like the sky while his hair was dark like a dense forest. "Comely for a servant." His eyes traveled down her entire body and then back up to her face.

She wanted to bite off his head and had to keep from crying out. She wasn't used to being treated this way.

"Tell me your surname, and from where you come."

"I am Evelina du – Bisset," she said, almost telling him her real name.

"Du Bisset?" He wrenched his face. I've never heard that name before. What part of France do you come from?"

She came from Tarbes in the Languedoc region near Toulouse but didn't want him to know. She also wanted to find out where he was from before she answered.

"Where is your abode, Sir Claude?"

He dropped his hand to the side. "My, you are brash for a servant."

"I – I'm sorry, my lord," she stammered, thinking she pushed it too far. "I just meant, I've never heard of you and wondered where you resided."

"I am Sir Claude Montague of Stonebury Castle in the north of France."

"Oh. I come from the southern part of France," she said, hoping he wouldn't ask her more.

"My lord," said the man's squire, running on foot, entering the courtyard out of breath. "I have your present for your sister in the travel bag and forgot to give it to you. I hope it's not too late."

"Nay, Felix," he said, thankfully taking his attention away from Evelina. "However, if I don't get into the great hall soon, I'm sure my sister will be hunting me down to retrieve her present."

"Come," said Rose, taking Toft's hand and heading toward the keep. "Claude, you'll want to greet Lord Nicholas and his wife, Muriel, I'm sure. You should see how tall the twins, Nelda and little Nicholas, got in the past few years. They are eight now, and little Nicholas is already a page."

"My, that time went fast," said Claude.

"They have more children as well," Toft told him. "Another boy and two more girls that are named Holly and Heather."

"Holly and Heather? What kind of names are those?" Claude asked, making a face and shaking his head.

"I think those names are pretty," Evelina blurted out, not able to stop herself from saying what she thought.

Claude looked over to her and narrowed his eyes. "Nursemaid, I was talking to Lady Rose and Sir Toft, not you."

Evelina felt outraged but couldn't say anything. She was supposed to be a servant but, at times like this, it was challenging.

"I like the names, too," said Rose.

"How could you?" asked Claude. "I think Lord Nicholas has been letting his wife influence his decisions. What is their other son's name? Clover? Or perhaps Dan – delion," he said with a chuckle.

"It's Glen," Rose told him.

"Of course," said Claude with a nod. "A glen for all those flowers."

"What is the matter with you, Claude?" asked Rose. "My name is a flower. Do you think my name is silly, too?"

That shut him up, and Evelina was happy it did.

"Nay, of course not," Claude apologized. "I'm sorry if I sounded blunt. I am only tired from the journey and not thinking straight, that's all."

"Let's get you a big tankard of ale," said Toft. "I'm sure that will fix you right up." Toft put his arm around Claude's shoulder, walking with him on one side and Rose on the other. Evelina followed behind them with the squire.

"Lord Claude seems very uncomfortable," Evelina stated, hoping to find out more information about the man through his squire.

"Oh, that's just because he is still in love with Lady Rose," blurted out Felix.

"I can see that. What I don't understand is how Lady Rose could have been in love with someone like Lord Claude. He is handsome but not very likable at all."

"Don't let him hear you say that," warned Felix. "Lord Claude had a hard life. Did you know when he first came to England and met his father, Lord John thought he was a girl?"

"A girl?" She giggled, letting her eyes roam over to the back of Sir Claude. The man was well built with broad shoulders and looked to have muscles under his tunic and cloak. He wasn't as tall as some of the other knights she'd seen, but he was still a good two heads taller than her. His face was covered with a dark stubble of whiskers. "It is hard to imagine that Sir Claude once looked like a girl."

"I've been told Sir Claude was very skinny and soft-spoken," the squire explained. "His hair was long and kept getting in his eyes. Supposedly, his own father took his blade to Claude's hair because everyone kept calling him a girl and John didn't want a son that they thought was a daughter."

She giggled again, and Claude turned his head, looking back over his shoulder.

"Is something funny?" he asked. "Mayhap you would care to share it with the rest of us?"

Evelina looked at Felix and shook her head slightly. "Please, don't tell him," she whispered, not thinking Claude would appreciate his squire revealing all his secrets.

"Nay, my lord," answered Felix in a loud voice. "I am just making conversation with the nursemaid. Evelina is very nice. And also pretty."

"Why thank you," she told him.

"Evelina is a lovely name," said Felix. "It suits you."

"Thank you, once again."

Claude looked over his shoulder for the second time. Evelina couldn't miss the scowl on his face. Something about Felix complimenting her and making her laugh seemed to upset him. Was there nothing that made this man merry?

"Felix, hurry to the great hall and find my sister. Tell her I will give her the present now," Claude commanded.

"Aye, my lord. Right away," Felix answered. Then he looked over to Evelina and winked, holding a finger to his lips. She giggled again as he ran off to the great hall.

Watching him go, she paid little attention to where she was walking and crashed right into someone. Putting out her hands to steady herself, she looked up to find she was touching Sir Claude's chest. His arms wrapped around her and he glanced down at her with partially hooded eyes.

"Sir Claude! I didn't see you," she said, stepping back and straightening her gown.

"You are not very trained in your duties, Nursemaid."

"What do you mean?" she asked him.

"You giggle at silly compliments and are not even aware where you are going."

"I didn't think Felix's compliments were silly at all. And it wasn't the compliments that made me giggle. I am sorry I crashed into you, but the last I knew you were headed for the great hall."

"Well, I changed my mind as well as my direction. Does that bother you?"

"Nay, my lord. It just surprises me that a man can't make up his mind. After all, that is more of a trait of a . . . girl." She giggled again and stepped around Claude, hurrying to catch up to Lady Rose.

CHAPTER 3

Second in Command

"Thank you for my doll, Claude." Charlotte reached up and kissed her brother, holding tightly to the rag doll he had given her for her birthday. It was dressed in a velvet gown that looked like a lady's. It even had a golden cloth crown sewn to its yarn-covered head.

"Please, everyone be seated as the meal is about to begin," announced Conlin, lord of the castle. Claude looked up to the very crowded dais table. There was an empty seat next to Rose, and she was waving him over. Toft sat at her other side.

"You'd better hurry, my lord. They want to start the meal," Felix told him.

Claude groaned inwardly. He didn't want to sit next to Rose because it was too much to bear.

"I would rather sit below the salt right now," mumbled Claude.

"Ah, I see," said Felix. "Too hard sitting on one side of Lady Rose while her husband is on the other?"

"Something like that." Claude dragged a hand through his hair wondering why he had ever come back to England after all. How was he going to endure the fact that Rose wanted him at her side every minute of the day?

"You can always sit down here with me," offered Felix. "I'll be eating with the nursemaid, Evelina." He nodded toward the table.

Evelina sat on the bench, not talking to anyone. The children of the nobles were all up at the dais with their families and she had nothing to do. She didn't seem to have any friends, either.

"What did you say to her earlier?" he asked.

"To Evelina?" asked Felix.

"Yes, Evelina. Tell me what you said that made her laugh."

"I was just rambling on, my lord. Sometimes it's hard to remember what I said."

"She commented on me changing my mind." His eyes drilled into her although she didn't know he was watching. She daintily broke off a small piece of bread, dipped it in her soup and brought it to her mouth. Then she proceeded to take a little square of cloth from her pocket and dab at the corners of her mouth. Odd, that a commoner acted so refined.

"Really? What did she say?" asked Felix.

"She compared my indecision to . . . to that of a . . . girl."

"Oh," said his squire, swallowing hard. "Perhaps I rambled on too much about your earlier years. I'm sorry, my lord."

"God's eyes, please don't tell me you told her that everyone used to think I was a girl?"

"Well, not exactly everyone. But I might have mentioned that your father thought so."

"What is the matter with you, Squire? I told you that in confidence. If I wanted the world to know, I would have had the herald shout it from the battlements. When I went back to France, I thought I left those and other memories behind."

"She looked lonely and I wanted to make conversation."

"Well, couldn't you have talked about the weather instead?"

Felix made a face and shrugged his shoulders. "She asked about you, my lord. I only thought it polite to answer."

"She asked about me?" Claude tore his eyes away from the girl and stared down at his squire. "What did she want to know?"

"It's hard to remember." The squire's eyes roamed over to Evelina. When Claude glanced back to her, she was smiling at Felix and waggling her fingers in the air. Felix smiled and waved back to her.

"Then think harder," Claude growled. "I want to know what she said about me."

"I believe she mentioned you looked uncomfortable. I

told her that was only because you were around Lady Rose and used to be in love with her."

"You didn't." Claude squeezed his eyes closed, feeling things going from bad to worse.

"It's not as if everyone doesn't already know you are still in love with Lady Rose."

Claude's eyes popped open. "What do you mean? I'm not still in love with her. That is in the past."

"Evelina didn't seem to think so. Girls can tell those things, I guess. She was surprised that Lady Rose could have ever been in love with you in the first place."

"Rose wasn't in love with me," he grunted. "And what do you mean Evelina was surprised by that? Is it that unbelievable that it could have ever happened?"

"Nay. Of course, I don't think so. But Evelina said even though you were handsome, she couldn't believe anyone could ever be in love with you because she said you were not likable at all."

"Not likable?" His eyes flashed over to Evelina. She was watching him, but when he caught her eye, she looked the other way. "How can she say that? That is preposterous. I'm likable. Everyone likes me. How can anyone think I am not likable?"

"Excuse me, my lord," interrupted a young page.

"What do you want?" snapped Claude. The young boy jumped.

"My name is Nicholas Vaughn. My father said he knows you. He sent me over to get you. He said the meal is starting and you need to join the nobles at the dais."

"I'll go when I'm ready to go."

Felix cleared his throat. "Likable, my lord. Likable," he mumbled.

"Oh." Claude realized he snapped at the boy and now felt horrible about it. He had been so upset at hearing that the nursemaid thought he was unlikable and that she knew he used to look like a girl, that he couldn't think straight. "Tell your father I will be there presently." Claude looked up and nodded to Lord Nicholas who raised a tankard of ale in the air and nodded back to him.

"Yes, my lord." The boy ran off.

"So, you won't be sitting below the salt with us, then?" asked Felix.

Claude studied Evelina. She was using the side of her spoon to cut a piece of chicken into smaller portions. Most of the servants he knew gobbled down their food quickly, using their hands and no spoon at all. They were just happy to have something to eat and eager to get back to work. She looked as if she were separating the food on her trencher into neat little piles before she even took a bite. This girl was like no other servant he'd ever met.

"Nay, I'll not be sitting down here with the servants. I am a noble and will sit at the dais, no matter how unlikable I am."

"Aye, my lord. I understand."

"Felix, keep an eye on that one," he said nodding toward Evelina.

"What do you mean, my lord?"

"There is something odd about her."

"I think she is delightful to be around." Felix smiled at Evelina. "She is stunning, too."

"And she smells like rosewater instead of sweat and tallow."

"Pardon me?" asked Felix.

"When she crashed into me in the courtyard, she was close enough that I smelled rosewater on her. I also noticed her hair was clean and not tangled at all. It smelled like fresh air. I think she is not who she pretends to be."

"Who do you think she is?"

"I'm not sure. I need to think about it. She seems familiar, but I don't remember anyone named du Bisset in France at all. I don't think that is her real name."

"So, she is hiding something?"

"I would bet on it. I wouldn't trust her at all. Keep your ears and eyes open and report back to me if she says or does anything suspicious at all."

"Aye, my lord. I will stay close to her at all times. It would be my pleasure."

"Not too close," Claude mumbled, walking away. "And stop telling her anything about me. If she wants to know something, tell her she can ask me herself."

EVELINA TRIED to listen to Claude and Felix's conversation, but there was way too much noise in the great hall to make out what they were saying. She had seen them looking at her several times and got the feeling they were talking about her.

"Hello, Evelina," said Felix happily, squeezing into the empty spot on the bench next to her. "How is the food today?"

"We are sharing a trencher," she said pushing the old, stale piece of bread being used as a plate closer to him. "I found it a little challenging to cut the meat without cutting into the trencher, so I apologize for the mangled look of the bread."

"Oh, I don't mind," he said, digging into the food.

"I separated the food because I wasn't sure if you cared for steamed cabbage. I am not fond of it, myself. However, the root vegetables are delicious today. The meat is a little tough and needs more sauce, but that was all I could manage to get. Some of the men at the table are very greedy."

"Aye, it is always that way below the salt. If you were up at the dais where Sir Claude is sitting, you would have more than enough food to eat and have the first choice of the best cut of meat."

"Sir Claude," Evelina repeated, taking the wooden cup into her hands, looking over the rim as she took a sip of honeyed mead. Lady Rose smiled from ear to ear, holding up a piece of cheese to Claude's mouth. He shook his head and flashed a smile, then buried his nose in a tankard of ale. "He is an odd one, isn't he?"

"That's funny," said Felix, using his fingers to shove more food into his mouth. "He said the same thing about you."

She jerked in surprise. "He did? He thinks I'm odd? How so?"

"He said you don't act like any servant he's ever known."

She put down the cup, almost spilling the mead in the process. She needed to be more careful with her disguise. "What else did he say about me?"

"He said if you want to know anything about him that you should ask him instead of asking me."

"He did, did he?" She used the spoon and scooped up a cooked piece of carrot, gently placing it into her mouth and then using the scrap of cloth to wipe her lips afterward.

"Just like that," said Felix, nodding to the cloth.

"Like what?" she asked, neatly folding the cloth into a square and slipping it back into her pocket.

"He has never seen a servant use a cloth to wipe her mouth. He also said you are too dainty to be of peasant stock. And you smell like rosewater, and your hair is clean and smells like fresh air."

"I smell like rosewater?" Her heart skipped a beat. Sir Claude noticed that she'd used a small dab of Lady Rose's rosewater. She liked that he was so observant, but it frightened her at the same time. He was going to figure out her secret. Being from France, he could send a missive back to her father. If so, before she knew it, she'd be marrying the awful Lord Onfroi. She needed to be more careful around this French knight.

When the meal ended, there were games for the children to help celebrate the birthdays of Harry and Charlotte. Evelina went to help the children, hoping someday she would have children of her own.

The children played several games, and the last one had to do with balancing eggs on spoons as they hurried across the great hall, walking around a few obstacles and then back again. The minstrels in the gallery overhead played music. When the music stopped, they had to run back to the start with their egg, hoping not to drop and break it.

"It's your turn, Harry," said Evelina, helping the little boy balance his egg on a spoon. "You need to beat Charlotte if you want to win the race."

"Charlotte, let me help you with that," said Claude, making his way down the dais to help his sister.

"I don't need help, Claude," Charlotte told him. "I'm eight now and old enough to play the game by myself."

"Hello, Evelina," said Claude, looking straight ahead instead of at her when he spoke.

"Hello," she said, looking down at Harry.

"Did my squire give you the message?"

"What message?" she asked, pretending not to know. It would be better if he didn't realize she had been talking about him.

"Didn't he tell you? If you want to know anything about me you are to ask me directly, not go through him."

"There is nothing about you I have the desire to know."

The music started up, and Evelina urged Harry forward. "Go on, quickly," she told him, clapping her hands together. "But not too quickly or you will drop the egg."

"Hurry, Charlotte." Claude put his hands to his mouth to call out to his sister. "You need to beat Harry. Show him that the de Bars are not losers."

"De Bars?" Evelina stood up so quickly at hearing him say that name that she lost her balance and almost fell. He grabbed her by the elbow and steadied her.

"Careful," he told her. "You might hurt yourself."

She, along with everyone in France knew about the old man, Lord Pierpont de Bar who had watched his wife burn at the stake because she was accused of being a witch. Hadn't the squire said something about Claude's grandmother burning at the stake? It was also said that the de Bar family was cursed and some of the relatives were witches. Could he be part of this family? "Why did you say de Bar?"

"I said Montague," he told her.

"Nay, you didn't. I distinctly heard you say de Bar. Are you a de Bar or aren't you?"

"I told you, I am Sir Claude Jean Montague, but thank you for asking."

"That's a lie," she said under her breath.

"What was that?" asked Claude.

"I said that's a tie. It looks like the race is going to be a tie."

"That's not what you said."

"Of course, it is." She looked directly at him and smiled.

The crowd cheered for the children as the music stopped. Charlotte and Harry both ran back to the start, somehow managing to keep the eggs balanced on the spoons. Harry crossed the line at the same time as Charlotte.

"You won, Charlotte! Congratulations, Sister." Claude scooped her up, causing her egg to drop to the ground and break. "You should be proud to be a Montague." He looked at Evelina as he said it.

"Harry crossed the line at the same time as Charlotte. Just like I told you, the race was a tie." Evelina picked the boy up in her arms and held him to her chest.

"My brother said I won," shouted Charlotte.

"Nay, I won." Harry looked like he was about to cry.

"It's all right, Harry. Better luck next time." Claude reached out and ruffled the little boy's hair. Harry opened his mouth and let out a wail.

"Harry doesn't like anyone ruffling his hair," Evelina told Claude.

"It's just my way of showing affection," said Claude. "There is no harm done."

"Then, mayhap, you'd let Harry return the same affection by ruffling your hair as well. Unless that would bother you."

"Why would it bother me?" asked Claude. "As I said, it is all done in fun. Go ahead, Harry. Ruffle my hair." Claude leaned over. Evelina urged the little boy to do the same to Claude as he had done to Harry.

With tears in his eyes, Harry slapped his hand atop Claude's head. However, the egg was in his hand and it broke on Claude's head. Slimy egg white and yolk slid down Claude's hair and face.

FORBIDDEN

Evelina giggled while Claude clenched his jaw, not saying a word.

"Oh, Harry, what did you do?" Rose rushed over with Toft, eying up the antics of her little brother. Isobel hurried over with Claude's mother as well.

"Claude, you have egg on your face," said Celestine.

Suddenly, all the children were crowding around, and everyone, including Rose, laughed at Claude. Claude wiped the egg out of his eyes and licked his lips.

"I'll have a tub of water sent up to your solar for you, Claude," said Rose. "I'm sorry that Harry did that."

"Harry was only ruffling Claude's hair as Claude did to him," stated Evelina. As everyone continued to laugh, Claude's gaze met with Evelina's. The anguish and despair in his eyes told her that this situation had hurt him deeply.

"Excuse me, my lady," Claude said, bowing to Rose with egg still dripping down his face. "I think I will retire for the evening."

Claude hurried through the great hall with his squire at his heels. No one but Evelina seemed to notice the turmoil on Claude's face. Her heart went out to him. It was her fault since she'd told Harry to ruffle his hair. Now, she regretted her action. It wasn't anger she viewed in Claude's eyes as he hurried away. It was pain. A more profound pain than she'd ever seen in anyone's eyes before. She wanted to run after him and tell him she was sorry, but couldn't. She was only a servant, she reminded herself. She couldn't step out of line again or her secret might be revealed.

Every part of her wanted to comfort Claude and make

him smile. Why did she feel this way when everything the man had done so far had been nothing but belittling to her? Then again, his actions were typical for a nobleman and the way they treated servants. Her actions were not normal for a servant, just like Claude had told his squire. Pretending she was someone that she was not was becoming more difficult all the time.

CHAPTER 4

Second in Command

Claude dipped his head under the water of the tub and broke the surface with a sigh. The hot bath felt inviting but was doing nothing to make him feel better. The nursemaid had made him look like a fool in front of everyone, especially Rose. It brought back too many hurtful memories of the past.

He was a knight now and wanted to leave the past buried of the days he was a frightened, angry, skinny boy with long hair in his eyes. He wanted his father to be proud of him. Hell, he wanted to look good in Rose's eyes now that he could measure up to someone like her husband. But Rose laughed at him, and that only made him want to try harder to make her like him more.

Was he really unlikable? He scooped up some soft soap from a small dish hanging from the edge of the tub and scrubbed his body hard. He wanted people to like him. Too much of his life was spent feeling lonely, and he didn't ever want to feel that way again.

A knock sounded at the door. He figured it was either his squire coming back with more wine or a servant bringing the towel they had forgotten to leave.

"Enter," he called out, scrubbing the soap into his scalp and closing his eyes, dipping back under the water to rinse it.

Evelina clutched the towel in her hand, glancing down the corridor, hoping no one was watching. She had intercepted the servant and told the young boy she'd take the towel to Lord Claude. She wanted to talk to him alone and try to find out if he had any suspicion of whom she really was. This was the only way to do it.

Hearing Claude call out to enter, she nervously reached out for the door handle, hesitating a second, and pulling her hand back. He might already be in the tub. If so, she would be in the room with a naked man. Then again, perhaps he was fully dressed and waiting for the towel and hadn't even entered the tub yet.

She heard voices down the corridor and quickly reached out and turned the handle, slipping into the darkened room so she wouldn't be discovered. Silently closing the door, she took a minute for her eyes to get accustomed to the dark. There was a fire on the hearth and one small candle burning on a table near the bed.

Evelina scanned the room, seeing the tub of water, but

not seeing Claude anywhere. She thought that mayhap she had imagined him telling her to enter and perhaps he wasn't here at all. She turned around to leave and heard the sound of water splashing over the edge of the tub onto the floor.

"Bring me the towel quickly, servant. I have soap in my eyes."

She spun around to see Claude standing up in the tub, rubbing his closed eyes. His naked, toned body glistened in the firelight as rivulets of water trailed down his sturdy chest, disappearing into the thatch of dark, curly hair at his groin. She lifted her hand to block her eyes from looking any further. She shouldn't have entered the room after all.

"Hurry, give me the drying cloth," said Claude, holding out one hand.

With her eyes turned downward, she slowly walked toward the tub, stretching to give it to him.

"Where is it?" he asked, his hand grasping at thin air.

"It's right here," she said, pushing it into his grip.

His fingers closed over her wrist and he pulled her to his chest. The air whooshed from her lungs and she crashed up against his naked, wet body.

"I might have soap in my eyes, but I would know that voice anywhere," he growled. With one hand, he wiped the water from his eyes, still holding her wrist with the other.

"Let go of me," she demanded, feeling her heart racing in her chest.

"Are you sure that is what you want, Nursemaid?" He put his mouth right next to her ear, causing her to shiver.

"After all, the only reason I can see that a nursemaid would enter my chamber when I'm naked is that she wants to give me more than just a towel, if you know what I mean."

"I'm sure I don't know what you mean," she said, struggling against his hold, looking at the ground rather than looking at his naked body.

He ripped the towel from her hand and released her, sending her stumbling backward.

"Don't worry; I am not interested in bedding you." She heard the splash of water and then the rustling of the cloth. When she daringly looked up, he had stepped from the tub and had the towel tied around his waist. "So, don't waste your time trying to get my attention because you are the last person I would ever take to my bed."

That infuriated her. It was bad enough that he assumed she was there to throw herself at him. But now, he had to insult her by saying he didn't want her?

"I assure you, having a tryst with you was the furthest thing from my mind when I entered the room."

"Really?" He lifted a brow and cocked a lopsided grin. "Then what did you come here for, Nursemaid? To help scrub my back?"

"Nay!" she shouted. "I came here to apologize for what happened in the great hall."

"Why should you apologize?" he asked. "It was the boy who did it."

"Harry was only acting on my suggestion. If I had never told him to ruffle your hair, none of this would have happened."

"Aye, that's true." He picked up a wooden goblet on the table, trying to get the last drop of wine from the vessel. "Where is that squire of mine?" he spat. "Mayhap, you should have brought wine along with the towel. Why didn't you?"

That took her by surprise. "Mayhap, I shouldn't have ventured into your room at all. You sound so ungrateful."

"Oh, I'm sorry." He put down the cup and took a few slow steps toward her. "Am I being . . . unlikable?"

She swallowed deeply, not liking the way he almost seemed to stalk her. By the rood, he knew what she'd told the squire. "Nay, my lord. Not at all," she said, dropping her gaze to the floor.

"If I'm not unlikable, then why don't you look at me, Nursemaid?" He lifted her chin with his palm and, ever so slowly, she raised her eyes until she was gazing right into his swirling blue orbs. The sadness she'd seen earlier was gone. Replacing it was mischief and if she wasn't mistaken, a bit of lust as well. "What was the real reason you came here tonight?" he asked her.

"I told you," she said in a soft voice. "I came here to apologize."

"I don't believe that is entirely true." His eyes focused on her lips as he leaned in closer. "Then again, I don't believe you are who you claim to be, either."

"Y – you don't?" Her eyes fell to his mouth as well. "Who do you believe I am, my lord?"

She could feel his hot breath on her when he spoke. Her tongue darted out to wet her parched lips. He was going to kiss her, she was sure of it. This handsome knight was going to give her a sensuous kiss, and she welcomed it. Evelina closed her eyes and let her head fall back, waiting for the feel of his mouth pressed up against hers. Would the kiss be quick or long and drawn out? Would it be filled with lust and hunger or, perhaps, instead, filled with love and passion? She had to know.

He released her, never touching her mouth with his. "I think it is time for you to leave now, Nursemaid."

When she opened her eyes, he had turned and was walking away. He dropped down on the bed, lounging back, raising his arms behind his head to use as a pillow. Now she was the one who felt like a fool, standing there with her head back and eyes closed waiting for a kiss like a lovelorn adolescent. In worrying about the pain and turmoil she'd caused him, she'd release the wrath of displeasure upon herself. This wasn't at all what she had expected.

"Why are you still standing there?" he asked. "I told you I don't want you in my bed, so why don't you understand that?"

"You are a wretched cur, no different than any other man I've ever met."

He released a deep chuckle. "I'm sorry if I am not living up your expectations, but I am not used to having a woman play the aggressor. I suppose if you are adamant about staying here, I can make an exception. It has been a while since I've bedded a servant."

"How dare you!" she blurted out, no longer caring that

she was not acting like a servant. This man made her blood boil, and she was not going to put up with his rudeness. Even if she were a servant, he had the manners of a pig!

His smile disappeared and he pushed up to a sitting position, watching her intently.

"I should report your actions and your brash words to Lady Rose immediately."

"Your threats don't frighten me because I know you would never do it."

"Why would you say that?" He scooted to the edge of the bed.

"Sir Claude, my only reason for coming here tonight was because I felt sorry for you."

"Sorry for me?" Anger flashed in his eyes. "I don't need your pity. And neither do I know what you mean."

"I saw the pain in your eyes when everyone laughed at you in the great hall. I especially noticed your despair when Lady Rose laughed at you as well. It hurt you, didn't it?"

"Who are you to ask me such a question?"

"You care what she thinks about you and are trying your hardest to leave a good impression."

"I don't need to impress anyone," he scoffed.

"You don't. Yet it means everything to you that Lady Rose sees you in a light that matches that of her husband. Doesn't it?"

"Stop it!" he commanded.

"You wouldn't want her to know I was in your solar while you were naked because she might think you are a cur instead of the honorable knight you want her to believe you are."

"I am an honorable knight and not you or anyone else can say differently."

"Really?" It was her turn to raise a brow. "Suppose I go to Lady Rose right now and tell her that I came to apologize to you and you tried to kiss me, seduce me, and take me to your bed?"

"You wouldn't!"

"You wouldn't like that, would you? Because if so, you would never get Lady Rose to love you the way she loves her husband, Toft."

"Bid the devil, I will whip you if you say one more word." He stood up so quickly that his towel slipped from his hips, falling to the floor and leaving him standing in front of her, naked.

At the same moment, the door opened behind her, and his squire entered the room.

"My lord I have brought wine and – oh, I'm sorry. I didn't know you were in the midst of bedding a woman."

Evelina turned on her heel and ran from the room.

CLAUDE PICKED up the towel and wrapped it back around his waist. He sat on the edge of the bed with his head in his hands. What had just happened? And what had the nursemaid meant about him wanting Rose to love him the way she loved her husband? She didn't know what she was talking about. Or did she?

"Come in and close the door, Squire," he spoke into his hands. Ever since he'd arrived in England, things hadn't been going well at all. Why did every day have to be harder than the one before?

"What was Evelina doing in here?" asked Felix, closing the door.

"That's what I want to know," he replied. "She said she came to apologize, but all she did was say horrible things about me instead."

"Oh," said Felix, pouring a cup of wine and handing it to Claude. Claude took it and chugged it down, trying to use the alcohol to numb his mental turmoil. "Did she call you unlikable again, my lord?"

Claude didn't know how to answer. Evelina was right in saying he couldn't go to Lady Rose and tell her about this. After all, his squire had seen him standing there naked with the girl in the room. Who the hell knew who else saw it as they passed by in the corridor. It wouldn't paint him in a good light at all.

"Do you think I'm unlikable, Felix?" He held out his cup for more wine.

"Well, on occasion you do come across as, shall I say, grumpy?" Felix filled up the cup with wine and put the decanter on the bedside table.

"I'm not unlikable, and neither am I grumpy." He felt the frown on his face as he said it. "God's eyes, who am I fooling? The girl was right. I am unlikable. But she was wrong when she said I wasn't an honorable knight."

"She said that about you, my lord?"

"She did."

"Are you going to tell Lady Rose her servant is speaking out of line?"

"I'm not."

"You're not?" Felix scratched his head.

"Nay. Instead, I am going to prove to her, as well as to everyone else, that I am an honorable knight, and I am not a wretched cur nor am I a pig."

"Cur? Pig? Did Evelina say that about you, too?" Felix's eyes opened wide.

"It doesn't matter what she said because it is not true. She is only a servant and knows nothing at all."

"What are you going to do to prove it to her, my lord?"

"I am going to show her that I know how to treat a lady."

"Oh. Are you going to kiss her?"

"I am talking about a lady, Squire. Evelina is not a lady. She is naught but a servant who needs a good scolding if naught else. But I won't be the one to give it to her. I am here for Lady Rose at her request. From now on, I am going to be the most likable person in the castle. Lady Rose won't laugh at me ever again. When she has her baby, I will be at her side. I will be there to walk her to chapel every day and to escort her to the dais for every meal. I will treat her with kindness and respect, and show her the ways of courtly love, like the knights practice in France."

"Lady Rose? I'm confused. I thought we were talking about the nursemaid, Evelina."

"Evelina? Why would I care what she thinks? I told you, she is only a servant."

"But I thought you said you didn't think she was who she pretends to be. Perhaps, she is not a servant at all."

"I changed my mind. She might not be a nursemaid, but I assure you if she is anything else it is naught but a peasant or a ragpicker, disguising herself so that she can take up residence at the castle."

"So, I'm confused, my lord. Is it Lady Rose or Evelina you are trying to impress?"

"Impress? I am not trying to impress anyone," he said, holding out his cup for more wine. He said the words but, in his heart, he knew they weren't true. Evelina was right in saying he wanted Rose to love him. But the nursemaid confused him. She had him so disturbed that he couldn't think straight. After looking into her hazel eyes and getting lost in those little green specks, and smelling the damned rosewater on her skin, he almost kissed her. What was wrong with him? Girls like her were not what he wanted. He was a knight of a castle and lands now. What he needed was a noblewoman for a wife. Someone just like Lady Rose. Tomorrow, he would show everyone just how honorable a knight he could be.

CHAPTER 5

Second in Command

"My lady, how much longer will we be in England?" Evelina's guard, Augustin, asked her in the courtyard the next day, speaking French.

"Shh," said Evelina, looking over her shoulder at the crowd of people gathered around the gate. The lord of the castle and Lady Rose's husband were leaving along with a good amount of men to pay their service to the king today. "*Augustin, ne m'adressez pas en tant que dame,*" she said, telling him not to call her lady. "Someone might hear you." She pulled him into the shadows behind the mews to talk to him in private. They continued to speak in French.

"We've been here for a fortnight now," complained Augustin. "I need more money if you want me to stay here much longer."

"I've paid you well, and you are also getting paid to work as Lord Conlin's guard," she reminded him.

"I am a mercenary. I could be making twice as much back in France."

"We can't leave yet. I haven't found the man I want to marry."

"If you want me to stay to protect you and also keep your secret, you will have to give me more money."

She let out a deep sigh, reaching into her pouch for the few coins she had left in her possession. *"D'accord. Je te paierai plus d'argent,"* she told him, agreeing to pay him more money. She slipped the coins out of her pouch and dropped them into Augustin's hand.

CLAUDE ROUNDED the mews with his squire right behind him. He stopped dead in his tracks when he saw Evelina half-hidden in the shadows, giving a mercenary money. Felix crashed into the back of him since he stopped so suddenly.

"My lord. I'm sorry, I didn't know you were stopping," said Felix.

"Felix, look! I told you something was deceiving about that woman." He pulled Felix back out of sight, and they peeked around the side of the mews. "Did you see that?"

"See what?" asked Felix, stepping out to look, but Claude pulled him back into the shadows again. The mercenary went back up to the battlements while Evelina hurried to Rose's side at the front gate. "I can't see a thing," complained Felix, trying to see over Claude's shoulder.

"It was Evelina. I saw her giving that mercenary money."

"What mercenary?" asked Felix.

"Egads, Squire, try to keep up." Claude pointed at the mercenary climbing the battlements. "That one. She paid him coins."

"She did?"

"I also heard them speaking in French, which tells me they were trying to keep others from hearing their conversation."

"What did they say?" Felix stretched his neck, trying to get a look at the mercenary.

"I heard something about a secret. Then I thought I heard Evelina say she was going to pay him more money."

"What does that mean?" asked Felix. "Is she a whore?"

"Highly unlikely. If so, the mercenary would be paying her instead. Keep an eye on the mercenary and try to find out all you can. See if he'll tell you where he came from or why Evelina was giving him coins."

"Aye, my lord," said Felix, taking off at a brisk pace for the battlements.

Claude turned the corner of the mews and crashed into Evelina. He put out his hands and caught her by the shoulders.

"Watch where you're going, my lord," she said snidely.

"What were you doing behind the mews?" he asked.

"I could ask you the same thing."

"I was with my squire, coming to see the men off on their trip."

"What squire?" She looked around him but, of course, Felix was already gone. He didn't want to tell her he sent the boy to spy on the mercenary, so he decided to ignore her altogether.

"Lady Rose," he called out, leaving Evelina, hurrying to Rose's side.

"Sir Claude. There you are," said Rose, rubbing her belly.

"We need to leave, Toft," Lord Conlin called out from atop his horse. The other barons and their families had left earlier that morning.

"Ye are no' leavin' before ye give yer wife one more kiss," said Isobel, reaching up as Conlin reached down from the horse to kiss his wife. Their three sons gathered around her, bidding their father a safe journey.

"Goodbye, Father. Goodbye, Toft." Rose hugged and kissed her husband right in front of Claude. It made him very uncomfortable. He wished it was him she was kissing and hugging instead. He should be married to her right now instead of Toft.

"Claude," said Toft, clasping hands with him. "Can I count on you to watch over my wife until my return? Will you treat her as if you were me?"

"I will," said Claude.

He heard Evelina clear her throat, trying to say something without coming out with words. He could only imagine what message she was trying to give him.

The party left, and Rose wiped a tear from her eye. "Claude, I am so frightened to birth this baby without my husband or father here." She reached out and hugged Claude. He slowly put his arms around her.

"It will be all right, my lady. I am here and will serve you however I can. I will nurture you and protect you. There is no need to fear anything as long as I am at your side."

It felt damned good to hold Rose in his arms, although it was very awkward with her large stomach in the way. Thoughts flitted through his head of when he'd first met her. They were both so young. He was the one who needed comforting, being in a new land and finding out John was his father. He hadn't thought his parents were going to end up together. Neither did he think he would ever be the son his father wanted him to be. Rose had been there to support him. She had been the one to comfort him and encourage him, making him feel his life wasn't as awful as he thought.

Out of the corner of his eye, he saw Evelina holding Harry's hand. She had a smirk on her face, making him feel uncomfortable that he held Rose in his embrace. He couldn't help thinking of all the horrible things she said to him last night. She'd accused him of still being in love with Rose and wanting Rose to be in love with him as well. It wasn't at all the truth. Or was it? He released Rose and quickly stepped away.

"Claude Jean," called his mother. Celestine approached, holding Charlotte's hand. His father, John, was with them.

"Mother," he said, reaching out to hug her, just to keep away from Rose when Evelina was watching.

"Son, I have to leave for Winchelsea," said his father. He clasped hands with Claude and slapped him on the back to say goodbye.

"Safe journeys, Father."

"After Rose's baby is born, I want you to come to Winchelsea for a while," John told him. "You have yet to see the new castle. It is in the final stages of being built."

"I will," Claude promised. "I'd like to pay a visit to Hastings as well while I'm here."

"I'm not sure that is a good idea," John told him. "The ruins of Hastings Castle are only a reminder of a dreadful day. It upsets me still."

"I know it won't be easy, but that is where my grandfather lost his life. I would like to pay my respects," Claude told him. "Perhaps seeing it again will help me come to terms with what happened."

"You are a fine son, Claude," said his father with admiration in his eyes. "I am proud of you. However, I don't like the fact you have inherited your grandfather's demesne because it only takes you away from me. I feel as if I have already missed out on so much of your life. Will you ever consider making England your home? If so, I have a place for you in Winchelsea."

"I don't think so, Father. France is my home, and it is where I will stay."

"I understand." John's eyes held sadness as he said his goodbyes to Charlotte and Celestine, and rode out through the gate.

Leaving his father so soon after first meeting him at the

age of five and ten years old was not easy. Claude would have liked to spend more time getting to know the father he lived without for most of his life. John Montague might not have always been honorable, but he changed for the better after getting back together with Celestine. Claude didn't know how his mother ever worked through the hardships in her life. Being away from her, living in France, is one of the things Claude regretted.

"Ladies, I invite ye to join me in the solar to do some sewin'," Isobel told the noblewomen of the castle. "I am stitchin' a blanket for the new baby." Rose rubbed her hand over her stomach and smiled, looking downward. Claude had never seen the girl so happy in all her life. Her complexion almost seemed to glow.

"Claude, please come to the solar with me," Rose begged him.

"Me?" He looked around at the ladies of the castle watching him intently. His mother nodded slightly. They all seemed eager to have him there except for the nursemaid who was scowling at him.

"I have been feeling a few light pains," said Rose, rubbing her belly. "Oh, I felt the baby kick. Claude, you must feel this. You won't believe it." Rose grabbed his hand and laid it on her stomach, covering his hand with hers to hold it in place. Sure enough, Claude felt a kick against his hand and jumped back in surprise.

"Does the baby always kick that much?" he asked, having never felt anything like it.

Celestine laughed. "Claude, you kicked like a mule

before you were born. Your grandfather used to say that meant you were going to be trouble."

"Well, I hope this baby isn't any trouble," stated Rose. "Come along, Claude. You promised Toft you would be here for me, and I don't want you out of my sight until after I give birth."

Rose held on to his arm and started for the castle.

"Evelina, bring Harry to the ladies solar as well," said Rose. "He likes to play with the thimbles."

"Of course, my lady." Evelina followed at the other side of Claude, holding on to Harry's hand. Why did this make him feel so uncomfortable? It was bad enough that he had to be in the ladies solar instead of on the practice field with the men. But now, Evelina would be there watching his every move, giving him that all-knowing eye, trying to make him feel guilty that he was watching over Rose. Well, he was just going to have to show her that he was a knight doing his duty, at the service of Lady Rose, the daughter of the lord of the castle. There was naught to feel guilty about since he was only doing as asked by Rose and Toft.

EVELINA COULDN'T BELIEVE the way Claude doted over Rose, watching her every move. First, he gave her the sewing basket, and then he sat at her feet holding out his hands and letting her use them as spindles when she decided to wind yarn.

Most of the women were sewing and talking, but since Evelina was posing as a servant, they mainly ignored her. Harry fell asleep on a bag of wool the spinners used to make yarn for the tapestries. Feeling bored, she picked up a piece of stitchery and pushed the needle through the cloth, making small, beautiful stitches, following the pattern of flowers trailing across the bottom edge.

It felt good to be, once again, doing the actions of a lady. Being a servant was humiliating and much more work than she had thought it would be. Lost in her work, she jumped in surprise when Claude appeared from out of nowhere, bending over and whispering in her ear.

"For a nursemaid, you seem to know a lot about stitching."

"Oh, I was just trying it since Harry fell asleep. It looked like fun." She placed the stitchery down on the bench next to her, glancing up at Claude who towered over her.

"Really." He reached down, picking up the stitchery to inspect it. "I have never seen such small, elegant stitches before. Your work is accurate and surpasses the skill of any of the noblewomen. Where did you learn to do this?"

"I'm a fast learner," she said, hoping he wouldn't ask more questions. She had to turn the conversation around quickly. "I noticed you were very skilled in using your hands as spindles for Lady Rose's yarn." She stifled her giggle. He had looked so silly. A big, strong knight, playing handmaid to a lady was very funny, indeed.

"I am at my lady's service. No matter what she requests of me, I will do it. After all, I am an honorable knight, and it is my sworn duty."

"If you say so." She fussed with the wimple covering her head.

"Claude," called out Rose. "I feel like riding. Will you see to our horses anon?"

"Riding?" Claude stood up with a jolt. "Please beg my pardon, Lady Rose, but I am not sure it is a good idea in your condition."

"Aye, Rose," said Isobel. "Ye should no' be on a horse when ye are gettin' so near to givin' birth. Ye ken yer faither willna allow it."

"Isobel, my father isn't here to stop me, and neither is Toft. They have kept me from riding for months now, and I feel like I am going to go crazy if I don't get out. Claude will watch over me. There is nothing to worry about."

"I agree with Isobel," said Celestine. "I don't think you should go either. What if the horse gets spooked and throws you?"

"Rose, ye have already lost two bairns and canna risk losin' another one," Isobel warned her.

"I suppose you're right," said Rose with a sigh. She struggled to stand up. Claude shot across the room and was there at her side immediately. With his hand on her arm, he guided her, not letting go even when her balance was secure.

"Thank you, Claude. I am so glad you are here to help me." Rose covered his arm with her hand.

"It is my pleasure, my lady."

There was no mistaking the look of love in Claude's eyes. Evelina shook her head, getting to her feet as well.

Didn't the man realize how foolish he was acting? Perhaps, she would have to point it out to him again.

"If I can't mount a horse, then I want to ride in the wagon," Rose announced. "It is a beautiful day, and I would like to take a basket to the coast and sit on the grass as we eat the food. I long to walk barefoot along the shore and let the waves lap at my feet."

"Rose, that is no way for a lady to be actin'," Isobel reminded her. "How will it look if ye are seen with a man who isna yer husband and yer feet are bare?"

Rose chuckled. "I think the part that bothers you the most, Isobel, is the fact I will be shoeless. I doubt that you have ever been without shoes in your life."

"Isobel is right. You should stay at the castle," said Celestine. "You know your father doesn't like you anywhere near the docks."

"I won't be by the docks. I just need to get out in nature," said Rose.

"I will protect her, Mother," Claude told Celestine. "I am a knight now, not a boy anymore."

Celestine and Isobel exchanged glances. Isobel nodded, and Celestine smiled at Claude. "Of course, Claude. What was I thinking? I'm sure we have nothing to worry about if you will be with Rose."

"I will take the nursemaid with us so there will be no chance for idle gossip," said Rose.

"What?" Evelina looked up in surprise. The last thing she wanted was to have to go along as a spectator with those two. "I have to look after Harry," she said, splaying out her hand to the little boy sleeping on the bag of wool.

"We'll take my squire instead," Claude blurted out, giving a sideways glance to Evelina.

"I'll watch my son," said Isobel. "Evelina, ye go along with Rose in case she needs another female."

"Yes. We'll take your squire as well," Rose told Claude. "That way, Evelina will have someone to talk to."

The look of disturbance on Claude's face almost made Evelina laugh. But he didn't say a word against the idea. Instead, he forced a smile and patted his hand atop of Rose's.

"Whatever you wish, my lady," Claude answered. "I will have my squire make the preparations right away."

CHAPTER 6

Second in Command

𝒞laude directed the horse toward the coast. Rose sat on the bench seat next to him, looking as beautiful as ever with the sun making her golden hair glow. It was a sunny day and quite warm. A walk near the ocean would feel nice. Claude enjoyed his time alone with Rose, but what he didn't like was the fact that they'd had to bring his squire and the nursemaid along.

He glanced over his shoulder to see Felix sitting on the back of the open wagon, dangling his feet over the edge. Evelina sat with her back against the sidewall, clutching the basket of food in her arms.

"Where would you like to stop to eat?" Claude asked.

"Anywhere," grumbled Evelina. "It is so bumpy in the back of this cart it is making me feel ill."

"I was talking to Lady Rose," Claude told her.

"Oh." Evelina threw him a disgruntled look and turned her head the other way.

"Stop up ahead, just under that large tree." Rose pointed to where she meant. "It is where Toft and I often have an outing. I wish he could be here with us today, don't you, Claude?"

"Aye," he answered, hearing Evelina release a puff of air from her mouth from behind him.

Claude stopped the wagon and put his hands on Rose's waist to help her from the cart while Felix took the basket of food from Evelina and headed over to the big oak tree.

Evelina wasn't used to riding in the back of carts. She stood up just as the horse moved and she almost fell.

"Oh, Claude, help Evelina from the wagon as well," said Rose.

"I don't need help," she spat, taking a step forward, getting her foot caught on the hem of her gown and almost falling again.

"Squire, get over here and take care of the horse," Claude shouted, stomping over to the back of the wagon and holding out his hand. "Come," he told her.

"I said I don't need help," Evelina repeated.

"Lady Rose asked me to help you and so I will. Besides, if I don't, you might land flat on your face. You act as if you've never ridden in the back of a wagon before."

She had ridden in the front of wagons, but the back was always for servants. If her father knew she was dressed in a coarse, brown, woolen gown and riding in the back of a hay wagon, he would be furious. Then again, if he knew she was working as a servant, he'd be madder than hell.

She wondered if her father had his men out looking for her and how long it would take him to figure out she had stowed away with a mercenary to England.

"Come on," said Claude impatiently, closing his hands around her waist and lifting her from the cart.

"Oh!" she cried out, holding on to his strong shoulders so she wouldn't fall. He set her on her feet. When she looked up, he was staring down at her mouth. His hands lingered on her waist. Mayhap it was only her imagination, but she felt as if he wanted to kiss her. A shiver of desire swept through her. This was the second time he had touched her and, both times, she felt a heat spiraling through her with his contact. She didn't understand it at all. Memories of yesterday filled her head of how she thought he was going to kiss her then, too. Then she remembered how foolish she felt when he hadn't. She didn't want to go through that again.

Quickly removing her hands from his shoulders, she stepped back, biting her lip and looking at the ground. "Thank you," she said in a breathy whisper, barely able to talk.

"Of course," he mumbled. She thought he would leave her then but, instead, he stayed with her. Her eyes lifted in question.

"Was there something you wanted to say, my lord?" she asked, wondering why he hadn't walked away.

He hesitated before he answered. "Nay. It's just that you have a piece of straw in your hair." He reached out and plucked the straw from her unbound hair. The ride in the back of the wagon had been windy and she had lost her wimple. Then, the ribbon holding back her hair came untied, and she lost that during the ride, too. "That's better," he said, showing her the piece of straw and dropping it to the ground. The wind picked up and blew her hair across her eyes. To her surprise, he brushed the hair from her face, gently tucking a strand behind her ear.

Their eyes interlocked and at that moment, the world stood still. As she stared into his eyes, her heart beat faster. He was looking at her like a lover, not like a man who didn't want her in his bed. Perhaps, he had lied yesterday when he turned her away. But his eyes didn't lie now. What she saw was a man's interest in a woman, and it wasn't Rose. It was her this time. He skimmed his fingers lightly across her cheek as he moved his hand away.

"My lord," interrupted his squire, suddenly standing at their side. With the squire's presence, the moment was gone. "Lady Rose said to hurry before the ants figure out we have food."

"Aye," said Claude, clearing his throat and taking a step backward. "Tend to the horse, Felix. And if you want any food you'd better not tarry. After all, I've worked up quite an appetite and might eat it all myself." He hustled across the grass, making a beeline toward Rose.

"Aye, my lord," answered Felix, talking to Claude's back as he hurried away.

Evelina stood frozen for a moment, trying to decipher what just happened. Had she imagined that they'd shared an intimate moment? And why had she enjoyed it so much? She didn't even like Claude. He was an arrogant, pig-headed, ridiculous boy trapped in a man's body refusing to live in anything but the past.

She straightened her gown, brushed back her hair and pinched her cheeks for color. It never hurt to look good, even around wretched curs like Claude.

* * *

CLAUDE TENDED to Rose's every need as they ate their food sitting on a blanket on the ground. Felix and Evelina sat on the edge of the cart, chatting as they had their meal. Claude poured some wine into a cup, bringing it to his mouth as his eyes focused on Evelina. With her long, oaken hair loose and flowing in the breeze, she reminded him of a fae.

He hadn't wanted to help her from the wagon, but when he touched her body, something odd happened that he couldn't explain. That damned rosewater drifted from her body again, filling his head with thoughts of sensual pleasures like kissing her neck or possibly her lips. He had almost kissed her last night. When he stood so close to her and gazed into her beautiful eyes, he couldn't stop himself from reaching out and feeling her silken hair as well as her skin. Thank goodness, she believed he was only brushing the hair from her eyes.

"Claude? Claude?" Rose leaned forward and pushed her face up to his.

"My lady?" It took him a moment to realize he had poured the wine for Rose and was drinking it instead of giving it to her. "Oh, the wine. I'm sorry." He handed her the cup. She took a sip, smiling all the while.

"Why are you smiling so much?" he asked. He heard Evelina giggle and his eyes darted back to the cart. He wondered what Felix had said to her to make her laugh.

"She's pretty, isn't she?"

"Pretty?" His eyes shot back to Rose. "Who?"

"Well, I'm not talking about Felix." Rose laughed this time, putting down the cup and reaching for her feet. "Claude, I want to walk in the water barefooted."

"Aye," he answered. He picked up the cup and drank the rest of the wine, sneaking a peek at Evelina again.

"I am having a problem reaching my feet."

"My lady?" He looked back at Rose, realizing she needed his help in removing her shoes. "Oh, I'm sorry, Rose. Let me help you." He reached out and slipped the shoes from Rose's feet.

"I'm glad you came to England because you are my good friend and I really missed you."

"Aye. I've missed you, too."

"I'm worried about you, Claude. Why aren't you married by now?"

"Me?" He looked up, holding her shoe in his hand. "I'll get married. Someday. When I find the right woman to be my wife."

"I had the feeling you left England because you were in love with me while I was in love with Toft."

He cradled the shoe in his hand, examining the stitches in the leather rather than looking at her when he lied.

"Nay, that's not why. My grandfather left me his castle and estate when he died. I had to go back to France."

"When you first returned, I thought, perhaps, you were hoping we could be together. But now I see that I was wrong."

"Rose, I have no idea what you mean."

"I think you do." She held out her arms. "Help me up, Claude. I feel like a whale."

He helped her to stand.

"Rose, I am here because you asked me to be. I want to help you any way I can."

"I saw the way you've been watching Evelina." Rose smiled a wide smile. "Perhaps, she is the one."

"The one? For what? The girl is a common servant with a brash disposition. I was only watching her because I thought someone should reprimand her before she gets out of control."

"Sure you were. Don't forget, now that the hair no longer hides your eyes, I can tell when you're lying."

"You and Toft asked me to stay and watch over you until his return."

"Aye. And I thank you from the bottom of my heart. We are good friends, and that is the way I always want it to be."

"What are you trying to say, Rose?"

"I'm saying that I'm in love with Toft and have always

been. He is my husband, and we will soon have a baby together. I hope to have many more babies with him."

"Why are you telling me this? I don't understand."

There was an awkward silence between them and then she shrugged her shoulders. "I suppose I am rambling on because I miss Toft and wish he were here with me when I give birth. But you are here, and that is the next best thing. Now, carry me down to the water because I should have waited to remove my shoes until after we were on the shore. I don't want to step on a stick or rock and stumble along the way."

"Yes, my lady," said Claude, scooping her up into his arms. He let out an involuntary groan, and that made them both laugh.

"Claude de Bar Montague, if I hear you groan again I am going to think you are telling me I've grown fat."

"Never, my lady," said Claude, carrying her down to the water.

"Where are they going?" Felix asked Evelina, causing her to look across the grass only to see Rose in Claude's arms. They were laughing as he carried her to the shore. Evelina had been having a pleasant conversation with Felix and enjoying herself. But now, all she wanted to do was go back to the castle.

"It looks like they are going to walk along the shore," she answered.

"That looks like fun. Let's go join them." Felix jumped off the wagon.

"Nay," she said, feeling her stomach form into a knot. "I'll stay here. I don't think I am up for a stroll along the beach."

Now, she realized she must have imagined that Claude was interested in her. He still loved Rose, and it was obvious. Never would she be fooled by him again.

CHAPTER 7

Second in Command

*C*laude tossed and turned all night long not able to sleep because of all the turmoil in his brain. First, he dreamed of Rose. He was her husband, and she birthed a baby boy that looked just like him. But in the dream, everyone kept thinking the boy was a girl.

After that, he dreamed that Evelina was in his bed and they were making love. Just as he reached his climax, her eyes lit up with fire and she slapped him hard, telling him he was naught but the court fool.

Finally, he had a dream about his grandfather. Claude was in the tower of Castle Hastings in the midst of a storm. His grandfather was there, telling him that he had to choose. He held up Rose by the hair in one hand and Evelina by the hair in his other hand. They dangled like limp rag dolls, and both of them looked blue in the face as if they were being hung by a noose. Claude stood frozen, not knowing what to do. Then the floor of the tower gave way under him, and he fell into a dark, long tunnel. He screamed out. But before he hit the bottom, someone's shout woke him from his sleep.

"My lord, wake up!" came his squire's voice. "You were crying out in your sleep."

Claude's eyes sprang open. He shot up to a sitting position in bed, gasping for air. Standing at the side of the bed were his squire and his mother.

"Claude, mon fils. Qu'est-ce qu'il y a?" His mother asked him what was the matter. She sat on the edge of the bed and put her hand on Claude's.

"Ma mère, j'ai eu un rêve horrible." He told her that he'd had a bad dream.

"I had a vision that you were in trouble, that is why I came to your room," said Celestine. "I didn't expect to hear you crying out in your sleep the way your father used to do with his nightmare." His mother often had visions and was very seldom wrong. She used her Tarot cards to tell the future but, to Claude, that was being a witch, and he wanted nothing to do with it anymore.

"It was just a dream," he said, throwing his legs over the side of the bed and rubbing his hands over his face.

"Felix, will you leave the room so I can talk to my son in private?" asked Celestine.

"Aye, my lady." Felix left the room and closed the door.

"Mother, if this is about my dream, you don't need to talk to me. I will be fine."

"Don't forget the dream your father kept having for years and what happened to him."

"I am not my father." He got out of bed and pulled a tunic over his head.

"Let me read the cards for you, Claude."

"Nay! I don't want anything to do with that type of witchery. Mother, it has only brought strife and turmoil into our lives."

"I suppose you are right." Sadness swept over Celestine's face. There was no doubt she was thinking about her parents and the horrible memories of her past. "You are acting strangely. Is something the matter? Does this have anything to do with your feelings for Rose?"

"Why does everyone keep saying that to me?" He continued to dress as he talked.

"Who else said it?"

"That nursemaid."

"Evelina? She knows you still have feelings for Rose as well?"

"I don't have feelings for Rose," he ground out, picking up his weapon belt and fastening it around his waist.

"Are you sure? Because you know she is in love with Toft, not you."

"Why does everyone have to keep reminding me?" He yanked his boots on and then headed for the door.

"Where are you going?"

"I am going to take Lady Rose to chapel for the morning mass and then to the great hall for a meal. And after that, I will rub her feet or brush her hair or do anything else she wants me to do, and no one is going to tell me otherwise."

"Why are you doing all this, Claude?"

"I am taking care of her until Toft returns, just as I promised."

"Are you sure that is the only reason?"

He stopped in his tracks and spoke without turning around. "I owe it to her, Mother. She brought me out of a dark place I was in many years ago. I owe everything to her. If she hadn't been there for me, I might be dead right now."

"It sounds as if you are placing too much importance on her random act of kindness. After all, your father is the one who saved your life and yet you very rarely spend any time with him."

His father. As much as Claude loved him, he still had a hard time accepting the fact at one time long ago his father left his mother and she had to raise Claude by herself. He barely knew his father since he hadn't met him until he was five and ten years of age. A father should be there for their children from the day they are born. He needed a father growing up and never had one until eight years ago.

"I am grateful Father saved my life. But remember, I haven't known him any longer than I've known Rose," he replied and headed out the door.

* * *

"My lady, I don't understand why you called me to your

chamber," said Evelina. "I should be taking care of the children and getting them ready for mass."

"Evelina, you won't have to worry about the children anymore," said Rose, struggling to get out of bed. Her late stages of pregnancy made it hard for her to move. Evelina hurried to her side to help her.

"What do you mean? And why don't you have a handmaid?" she asked.

"I sent my handmaiden home to tend to her ill mother a fortnight ago. Isobel has been helping me, but I think it is time for that to stop. You will be my handmaiden now."

"Me?" Evelina didn't want to do it. She was hoping to be able to make distance between her and Rose after yesterday. She didn't want to be around Rose or Claude because, for some reason, it bothered her to see them together. "I don't know anything about being a handmaid."

"There is nothing to know. I just need you here to help me dress. I can no longer reach behind my back, and it has been a long time since I have been able to touch my toes. I hope this baby comes soon because I've been getting fatigued. This will only be a temporary position until my handmaid returns in a week or two."

"That long?" asked Evelina, not even knowing if she was going to be in England for another two weeks. Any day now, her father could send a ship full of soldiers to look for her and then she would have no choice but to return to France.

There was a knock at the door, and Claude called out

from the other side. "My lady, I am here to take you to mass."

"Hurry, Evelina," said Rose. "Please, help me dress. I don't want Claude to have to wait."

"Of course," she said, hurrying to help her while Claude continued to pound on the door.

"Please, tell him we are going as fast as we can," said Rose.

"Aye, my lady." She pulled the gown over Rose's head and crossed the room to open the door.

Evelina didn't like being treated like a servant. She was a lady and should have servants waiting on her instead. Sadly, it was because of her own deception that she was in this position, and she tired of it quickly. She ripped open the door to find Claude with one fist raised, ready to knock again. His other hand was behind his back.

"We are going as fast as we can, now please stop the obnoxious pounding on the door," she grumbled.

"Evelina?" Claude raised a brow. "What are you doing here? Shouldn't you be with the children?"

"Not anymore. Lady Rose has made me her handmaid."

"Oh," he said, bringing his other hand from behind his back. He held up a bouquet of fresh wildflowers.

"What is that?" she asked. Her eyes focused on the beautiful flowers. The heavenly sweet scent filled the air.

"Flowers," he said, holding them out to her. "Here, take them."

Her hand shook as she collected the flowers from him, feeling her heart swell. No man had ever given her flowers before. She could barely believe it. Perhaps he was attracted to her after all.

"Put them in water for Lady Rose," he commanded. Stepping around her, Claude headed into the solar leaving her feeling, once more, like a fool.

* * *

BY THE TIME the morning meal ended, Evelina was so tired of watching Claude treat Rose like a goddess that all she wanted was to get far away from both of them.

He had brought Rose flowers this morning, stayed by her side during mass, and even cut her meat for her while sitting up on the dais with the rest of the nobles. She highly expected him to start kissing Rose's feet next.

The musicians in the gallery started playing dancing music. She looked up to see Augustin across the hall trying to get her attention.

After a quick glance around her to make sure no one was watching, she hurried across the hall to join him. Taking Augustin by the elbow, Evelina led him away from the crowd. She stopped in the foyer area leading to the outside.

"What is it, Augustin?" she asked. "I told you never to bother me in the great hall."

"I wanted to tell you I am boarding a ship back to France in the next hour. I found a merchant ship that is going that way, and I've secured passage for both of us."

"What? Nay," she said. "We can't leave now." Her

thoughts went to Claude. She didn't want to leave yet. She couldn't stop thinking about him, and she had even been dreaming about kissing him. Even though she had been feeling as if she wanted to distance herself from him, France was a little too far away. If she left now, her life would be over. As soon as she returned to France, her father would make her marry Lord Onfroi, and she would never have a chance to find love. She would also never know how it felt to kiss Sir Claude Montague.

"We must hurry because the ship won't wait," he told her.

"Augustin, I don't know."

"What don't you know?" asked Claude, showing up behind her. He must have seen her leave the room and followed her. "Mayhap I can help you decide."

Claude was the last person she wanted to see right now. To make matters worse, he overheard her conversation with Augustin. She was going to have to say something quickly to try to explain without giving away her secrets.

"This is Augustin." Evelina introduced the man to Claude.

"Yes, I know," answered Claude with a nod of his head. "Lady Rose said he is your brother. Funny, but he doesn't look anything like you. He is also much older than you."

"I could say the same about you and your little sister, Charlotte," said Evelina. "After all, you are fifteen years apart in age if I'm not mistaken."

"Hmph," Claude scoffed.

"My brother has secured passage on a merchant ship

back to France, but I don't think we should leave because I have a commitment to tend to Lady Rose until her handmaid returns."

"I'm sure Lady Rose can find another handmaid," said Claude.

"Yes, I agree." Augustin reached out and grabbed her by the arm and started pulling her out the door. "Let's go."

"Then again," said Claude, causing the man to stop. "Lady Rose is quite fond of Evelina, and it wouldn't be good to upset her since the birth of her baby is so close."

"Aye, I think you are right," Evelina agreed.

"I can't leave her here unescorted," snapped the guard.

"Unescorted?" asked Claude, sounding suspicious. "That is an odd choice of a word for a commoner to use."

"He just means that he's afraid for my safety," said Evelina.

"Oh, I see," said Claude. "There is no need to worry. I will watch over Evelina during her stay in England."

"Nay, that's not necessary," stammered Evelina, not wanting him watching her every move.

"She's not staying here." Augustin dragged her toward the door.

Claude took two long strides and gripped the man's wrist. "Get your hands off of her," he warned him. "I said I would protect her and it starts right now."

"I'm her older brother," growled Augustin. "She will do what I say."

"If you think I am daft enough to believe that story for one minute, you have another guess coming."

"We have papers to prove it," snarled the guard.

"Papers that are no doubt forged. I recognize you as a mercenary," Claude told him. "I believe I hired you a few years ago, and you told me you didn't have any family. Have you forgotten so soon, Augustin?"

The man's hand slipped off of Evelina's arm, but he stayed quiet.

"Evelina, you can stay if you want to, but I'm leaving." Augustin turned on his heel and headed out to the courtyard.

CLAUDE WAS glad to see the mercenary go. He'd been wracking his brain trying to figure out why the man seemed familiar. Then, when he saw Augustin pull Evelina out into the hall, it all came back to him. He was a mercenary and not a good one at that. Claude used him once, but when he found the mercenary stealing from his coffers, he let the man go. He really should have cut off his hand or hanged him, but that is not the kind of lord Claude wanted to be.

Claude had money. If the man had just asked, he would have helped him out. There were a lot of poor people that he'd helped over the years, even bringing the peasants into his castle walls for meals several times a week.

"Thank you," said Evelina once Augustin had left.

"Who are you?" he asked her.

"I told you. I am Evelina ... Evelina du ... de ... I'm just called Evelina," she answered, almost sounding as if she couldn't remember who she was.

"You told me your surname was du Bisset."

She looked startled when he corrected her.

"Yes, that's my name."

"Why are you lying to me, Evelina?"

"Lying?" Her face became red.

"I knew from the moment I met you that you weren't who you claimed to be. I have figured out who you are and why you came here from France, even though you won't tell me."

"Y-you have?" she asked.

"You are a merchant's daughter. Perhaps a spinster."

"Why would you think that?" She faked a laugh.

"I've seen the way you eat and the way you conduct yourself. You are certainly not a servant. I have also seen the way you stitch. It is as if you were born with a needle in your hand. That mercenary kidnapped you and brought you to England, trying to get ransom from your family, didn't he?"

"What? Nay. That's not true."

"Then there is only one other option."

"And what is that?"

"He was your lover."

"That is preposterous! He most certainly was not my lover."

"Then perhaps my squire was right. I saw you exchanging money with the mercenary. Mayhap you are a whore, and he wasn't satisfied and demanded his money returned."

That earned him a hard slap across the face. Evelina glared at him and stood with her hands on her hips looking as if she wanted to tear off his head.

"Don't ever speak to me that way again."

As she stormed off, Claude chuckled to himself. He knew the mercenary wasn't her lover and she was no whore. He only said it to get her flustered so she would hopefully tell him her true identity but it didn't work. Well, he'd find out who she was because now he was not only Rose's protector but Evelina's as well. The closer he got to her, the easier it would hopefully be to figure out why he was having these odd feelings for a mere commoner.

CHAPTER 8

Second in Command

*E*velina threw open the shutter and took a deep breath of fresh morning air. "My lady, it is time to awake so you are not late for mass," she told Rose.

Rose let out a soft moan and turned over in bed. "I am not feeling all that well today. I think I will stay in my chamber and not go anywhere."

"Lady Rose, is it the baby?" She rushed over to the bedside.

"I think I'm just tired, that's all." Rose pushed up to a sitting position in bed. The sheet slipped off of her, and the bulge of her stomach under her shift moved.

"I – I think I just saw the baby move," gasped Evelina.

Rose chuckled. "Yes, it is amazing. Here, give me your hand. You can feel the baby kick." Rose reached out, and Evelina stretched out her arm. Rose placed Evelina's hand on her large belly. "Right there. It should be any minute now."

A kick knocked against Evelina's hand, and her eyes opened wide. "I felt it. I felt the baby kick!"

Rose giggled. "You act as if this is the first time you've felt the kick of an unborn baby. Haven't you been close to anyone giving birth before?"

"Nay," she admitted.

"I thought since you are a nursemaid, you must have been present for many births when you were back in France."

"I . . . I wasn't always a nursemaid," she said. "The only time I've been around a pregnant woman was when my brother's wife and her baby died in childbirth."

"I see." Rose looked down at her belly and rubbed her hand over it in a loving manner. Suddenly, she seemed very sad.

"Oh, my lady, I am sorry." Evelina felt awful that she had just mentioned her sister-by-marriage dying in childbirth. "I am sure you will be just fine and so will your baby. I didn't mean to upset you."

"Nay, it is all right, Evelina. I was just thinking of the two babies I lost and was wondering what Toft would have done if I had died as well."

"Don't talk that way. Please," said Evelina, cradling Rose's hand in hers.

"Toft and I want a child desperately. My mother died in childbirth, and I lost five siblings as well, so I am very worried."

"I'm sorry, my lady. That is awful, and I am sure very hard to accept."

"Do you want children someday?"

No one had ever asked Evelina this before. She liked someone asking what she wanted in her life instead of telling her how it had to be. "Aye, I do," she said. "But I need a husband first."

"I'm surprised you are not married already."

"I want to marry someone I love. Just like you and Toft. I don't want to be married to someone just because my father wants me to be."

"Ah, now I understand why you left France. Your father wants you to marry someone, and you don't agree."

She looked down and wrung her hands in her lap. "I would rather not be married at all than to marry a horrible, mean man."

"I'm sure he's not as bad as you make it sound. Perhaps you should go back to your father and have a talk with him about this."

"Nay. I won't do that." She sprang up and paced the floor.

"What does your mother say about all this?"

"My mother is dead."

"I understand how hard it is for you. I lost my mother at a young age. I was so happy when Isobel came into my father's life because now I have another woman to confide in."

"So, you couldn't talk to your father about things either?"

"I blamed my father for my mother's death. But once I realized it was not his fault and how foolish I'd been, we became close. I can talk to my father about anything now."

"My father will never understand." Evelina shook her head in sorrow. "I need to find the man I'm to marry on my own."

"Claude is very nice. He is not married."

"Claude?" She spun around so fast that she almost fell.

"Mayhap, you should get to know him."

"He has been nothing but cruel to me," she told Rose.

"Claude? Cruel?" That made Rose laugh. "I honestly don't think the man has a mean bone in his body. You must have just started off on the wrong foot with him."

"Claude is a nobleman," Evelina reminded her. "I'm sure he would only consider marrying a noblewoman."

"I've seen the way Claude looks at you, Evelina. He has eyes for you even if you don't think so."

"Nay, that can't be. He is still in love with you."

"Me?" Rose stopped laughing and held her hand to her chest. "I'm married."

"I've seen the way he looks at you as well, my lady. I don't think Claude will ever marry anyone if he can't have you."

Rose's face became somber, and she nodded slightly. "I know what you mean, Evelina. I have noticed it, too, since he returned from France. But I have a feeling that is all going to change soon. We are only good friends. I am sure Claude knows it."

There was a quick knock at the door, and it opened a

crack. Rose's stepmother, Isobel, peeked into the room. "Are ye awake, Rose? If we are goin' to buy shoes in town, we will need to get an early start. I have a lot of shoppin' to do."

"Come on in, Isobel." Rose swung her feet over the edge of the bed.

"I thought you said you were feeling ill and tired and wanted to sleep some more." Evelina got the distinct feeling Rose had just been pretending.

"I am always tired, lately," said Rose. "However, I suddenly feel better." She looked over to Isobel with a wide grin on her face. "I'm never too tired for shopping for shoes."

Isobel and Rose giggled. Leaving the door open, Isobel quickly crossed the floor and sat down on the bed with Rose. "We are goin' to have to find a new place to hide the shoes or Conlin will have my head when he returns."

"Don't worry, Isobel. I will add them to the rest of the stash. Evelina, open that trunk in the corner."

"This one?" Evelina walked over to a trunk and lifted the lid. There was a baby blanket folded neatly at the top of the trunk. "Oh, what a beautiful blanket."

"I made that in the ladies solar. All the ladies helped to quilt it," said Rose. "But that isn't what I wanted to show you." Rose got up and walked over to the trunk along with Isobel. "Pick it up," she told Evelina.

Evelina picked up the blanket. To her surprise, the trunk was packed full of shoes.

"Shoes!" she said. "Lots of them."

"These are some of my favorites," said Isobel, picking up a pair of side-laced, soft, suede slippers with embroidered colorful stitching of flowers on them. "These look about yer size," said Isobel, perusing Evelina's feet. "I would like ye to have them."

"Me?" Evelina held her hand to her heart. "But . . . these are the shoes of a noblewoman. I am only a handmaid."

Rose and Isobel looked at each other, grinned, and then looked back to Evelina.

"We want you to have them," said Rose. "Mayhap, they will help you attract a husband."

Evelina reached out with a shaky hand, feeling very deceitful. How could she take such a gift when all she'd done was lie since she'd met these wonderful women? "I can't," she said, pulling back her hand. "Not until I tell you both something first."

"Good morning, am I missing something in here?" Claude walked in the open door and made his way over to the women.

Evelina groaned inwardly. She wanted to confide in the women, but she didn't want to tell Claude who she really was. If he knew, he would be sure to haul her back to France himself.

"You're not missing anything unless you'd like a pair of shoes, too," giggled Rose.

"Evelina was just about to try on her new shoes," Isobel told him. "Go ahead, lassie, put them on."

With everyone staring at her, Evelina had no choice but to try on the shoes. She decided she would tell Isobel and

Rose her secret later. She wanted to wait until Claude wasn't around.

"They fit ye like a glove," said Isobel.

"Yes, they do." Evelina lifted the hem of her skirt and admired the beautiful shoes.

"Don't they look good on her, Claude?" asked Rose.

"Huh?" Claude glanced down at the shoes and then back up to Rose. "Yes, I suppose so. Rose, are you ready? We are going to be late for mass."

"I'm not going," she said. "I am spending the day with Isobel. We are headed to town to shop."

"Not going to mass?" asked Claude in surprise. "Why not?"

"It is a pregnant woman's prerogative to change her mind, Claude."

"All right. I'll have my squire prepare the horse and cart, anon." Claude turned and headed for the door.

"You are not coming with us," said Rose.

Claude stopped and turned to face Rose with a perplexed look on his face. "What do you mean? You will need an escort. I am supposed to be watching you."

"My father's guard can escort us," said Rose. "I have another task for you."

"You do?" Claude furrowed his brow. "What could be more important?"

"I have a craving for rosemary and lavender soul cakes."

"Soul cakes? It's not even close to All Hallow's Eve," said Claude. "Where am I going to find those?"

"I know a woman who makes them fresh every day at

the White Cliff Inn," Rose informed him. "That is where you can find them."

"The White Cliff Inn," repeated Evelina. "Where is that?"

"It's in Dover," said Isobel.

"Dover is several hours' ride each way," protested Claude. "Can't you ask your cooks to make some here in Sandwich?"

"Oh, please, Claude," said Rose, rubbing her belly. "I have a craving for them. I am not sure the cooks here even have the proper ingredients to make them."

Claude sighed and then nodded. "As you wish, my lady. I will hurry and return to your side as soon as possible." He turned to go.

"My handmaid, Evelina, will be accompanying you."

"What?" blurted out Evelina and Claude at the same time.

"I'm in need of some new undergarments that they sell at the clothier's shop in Dover," Rose told them. "It is the only place I know of that sells clothes already made instead of making them to order. I wouldn't think of asking a man to purchase undergarments for a lady."

Rose looked over to Evelina and winked. Suddenly, Evelina knew where this was leading. Hadn't Rose suggested that Claude would make a fine husband for her? She squeezed her eyes closed, knowing Claude was going to protest.

"I don't suppose you can have your clothier make them here at the castle, can you?" asked Claude.

"These are already made and are some of the finest. I will give Evelina instructions as well as money to purchase what I need."

"All right," Claude agreed, causing Evelina's eyes to spring open. Where was the protesting of having her along that she expected? "But we're riding horses because a wagon is only going to slow us down. I will be back before sunset, Lady Rose."

Claude left the room. Evelina stood speechless, not knowing how to respond.

"Rose, I have a feelin' ye are no' really needin' soul cakes or undergarments at all," said Isobel. "What are ye up to?" She crossed her arms over her chest and looked at Rose from the corners of her eyes.

"Isobel, whatever do you mean?" asked Rose, walking over to the pouch of coins on the table and scooping it up, giving it to Evelina. "Here you go. That should be more than enough. Be sure to pick up a nice gown for yourself as well while you are at the clothier's shop."

"A gown? For me?" asked Evelina. Rose leaned in closer and whispered. "Claude likes the colors of blue and purple the best. And if you have a chance, get yourself a bottle of rosewater too. The scent of rosewater is one of his favorites."

Evelina gripped the pouch of coins tightly in her hand. Her heart beat faster. Thinking of being alone with Claude sent a spiral of heat surging through her. "How do I know what kind of undergarments to get for you?" asked Evelina.

"Oh, just get whatever you'd like. I trust your judgment." Rose swiped her hand through the air in a dismissing manner.

"Thank you, Rose," said Evelina, feeling uncomfortable. She couldn't take what was offered until she told Rose the truth. "I need to tell you something first. Once you hear what I have to say, you might change your mind."

"Evelina," came Claude's bellow from the corridor. He appeared in the open doorway with a scowl on his face. "God's eyes, what is taking you so long? We need to move faster. If you are going to be tagging along, I won't have you slowing me down. Do you understand?"

Evelina felt as if she were never going to be able to tell Rose the truth. She didn't move, not knowing what to do.

"Whatever you have to tell me can wait until later," Rose told her.

"That's right," said Isobel. "Now go on and get outta here so I can take Rose to town. Our shoes await us."

"Thank you," whispered Evelina, clutching the pouch and hurrying to join Claude.

CHAPTER 9

Second in Command

Claude hurried to the stables, glancing over his shoulder to make sure Evelina was keeping up with him. Bid the devil, why was Rose sending him on errands? That was what servants were for. Servants like the handmaid, but not nobles like him. He was supposed to be there to take care of Rose and protect her. He needed to be there for her when she birthed her baby. He didn't like the idea of being so far away.

"Squire, do you have those horses saddled yet?" Claude stormed into the stables.

"My lord, we are working on it," said Felix, saddling two horses with the stable boy helping him. "You just gave me the order not five minutes ago."

"Well, we've got to move fast," said Claude, reaching out and securing the straps on the saddle himself. "It will take a good part of the day to ride to Dover and back. I need to be here for Rose."

"She is in good hands with Isobel and your mother," Evelina told him.

"Rose is my concern," he said, securing the travel bag to the horse. "I promised her father as well as Toft that I would protect her and watch over her until they returned."

"Don't you think you are going a little overboard with all this?" asked Evelina. "After all, Rose is a grown woman. She's not the young girl you once knew."

"If you are going to be riding to Dover with me, I must warn you now; I don't like chatter."

"She's coming with us, my lord?" asked the squire. "Shall I saddle another horse, then?"

"There are no more available horses," the stable boy told him.

"What about that one?" asked Evelina, pointing to the only one left in the stall.

"That one is being used to pull the wagon to town," said the stable boy. "Lady Isobel told me to have it ready, so I need to hurry." The stable boy ran over to take care of the horse and cart.

"I suppose I could stay here," said the squire.

"Nay," said Claude, not sure he wanted to travel alone with Evelina. "Your place is at my side, Squire."

"But there are only two horses, my lord," said Felix. "Did you want me to run alongside as you ride?"

Claude shook his head. "Nay. That will take too long. The handmaid will have to ride with you."

"Evelina is going to ride with me?" Felix sounded much too excited at the suggestion. "I will hold you tight so you don't fall off the horse, Evelina." He leaned lazily on the stable door and smiled.

Claude didn't like the idea of Evelina riding with Felix now. He thought back to the other day when Felix and Evelina sat on the back of the cart together talking and laughing. He wanted Evelina to laugh and be lighthearted around him. Nay, this would never do.

"Get on your horse and stop gawking." He kicked the gate. When it swung, Felix fell to the ground. "The girl will ride with me."

"My lord?" Felix jumped up and brushed off his clothing. "But I thought you just said she was riding with me."

"I can see now that having her on your horse will only be a distraction. The way the two of you will be chattering away, it is sure to slow us down." He mounted the horse and directed it out of the stall. Then, reaching down, he extended his hand to Evelina. "Let's get a move on," he said.

EVELINA STARED at Claude's hand, not understanding at first what he wanted.

"Give me your hand."

"Oh," she said, tying the pouch of coins at her waist and reaching up, letting him help her mount. She plopped down across his lap in the sidesaddle position with both legs on the same side of the horse.

"Not like that," he grumbled. "Spread your legs."

"S-spread my legs?" she repeated, feeling that heat rising in her body again. Why had her mind wandered to wanting him to say that in bed?

"Ride like a man," he told her.

"I don't think I can."

"Then let me help you." He took hold of her gown and hiked it up to her knees.

Evelina reached out and slapped him.

"Bid the devil, if you don't stop slapping me every time you are near me, I swear I will tie you to a rope and pull you behind the horse instead. Now spread your legs."

Before she had a chance to object, he'd picked up her leg and placed it on the other side of the horse. She felt like a strumpet with her legs spread and her gown pushed up to her knees. Her bottom end was wedged in between Claude's legs and pushed up against his groin.

"That's better," he said with his mouth pressed up against the side of her head.

"I'm ready, my lord." Felix directed his horse out of the stable and Claude followed.

As soon as they got over the drawbridge, Claude directed the horse into a run. Evelina jerked and almost lost her balance.

"Don't worry; I've got you." Claude's arm slipped around her waist and pulled her closer to him. With his body pressed up against hers, she felt heady. Safe in his embrace, the wind blew her long tresses up into the air. With her eyes closed, she focused on the feeling of the warm sun on her face and the scent of Claude's leather doublet. It felt right to be in his embrace, and she couldn't stop wondering how it would feel to kiss him.

"You need to wear a wimple," he growled, bringing her out of her daydream.

"I lost it on our last ride and no longer have one."

"Well, get your hair out of my face. It is blowing into my eyes and mouth."

"So sorry, my lord." She reached up and pulled her hair to one side.

CLAUDE COULD BARELY CONCENTRATE on the journey with Evelina sitting wedged between his legs. With his arm wrapped around her small waist, he felt like he wanted to protect her as much as he did Rose. Her scent filled his senses, and her hair kept blowing in his face, embracing him in her essence of rosewater and fresh air.

He tried to sound gruff because he didn't want Evelina to know her presence was affecting him. Hell, he was even starting to feel randy with their bodies pushed together like this. Perhaps it wasn't such a good idea to have her ride with him after all.

And then she moved her hair to the side, exposing her long, smooth, milky-white neck. It took all of his control not to lean forward and kiss her. He already knew what her hair tasted like, but now he wanted to taste her skin and her lips as well.

They'd been riding for about an hour when he felt himself getting hard with the bouncing motion of her bottom end against his groin. If he didn't get away from her quickly, it was going to prove to be a very embarrassing situation for him.

"We'll stop to rest and water the horses just up ahead at that brook," he called out to Felix.

"Aye, my lord," said Felix.

"I am glad we are stopping because I need to use a bush," Evelina told him.

Claude stopped the horse and slid off before it even came to a complete stop. Then he reached up and put his arms around Evelina's waist, helping her dismount. With her hands on his shoulders, she slid down his chest. Claude was award of every womanly curve of her body against him and beneath his fingers. Then, she looked up, and he found himself falling deep into her bright eyes.

Sunshine illuminated her oaken hair as it lifted in the breeze. She was beautiful. Just as beautiful as any noblewoman he had ever known. Why hadn't he fully realized this before?

"I'll be right back," she said, turning and walking into the foliage. He watched her go, feeling the bulge in his breeches growing even more. Damn, he wanted her. By right, she was only a servant, and he was a noble. He could command her to go to bed with him and she couldn't deny him.

But Claude wasn't like that. He didn't possess the ways of his father or some of the other nobles. Nay, he had never taken any woman, not even a servant, to his bed without her consent. Bedding Evelina was out of the question. It was evident the girl didn't like him because she kept slapping him.

"Do you want me to tend to the horses, my lord?" asked Felix.

"Aye," he said. "I need a few minutes alone, so don't bother me."

"Of course, my lord."

Claude went down to the water to douse his face and, hopefully, extinguish the fire burning inside him. With Evelina along, this was going to be a very long trip.

CHAPTER 10

Second in Command

After stopping to water the horses, Claude had Evelina ride with Felix. She was a little disheartened and wondered why. He had also been adamant that she ride behind Felix instead of in front of him.

"This is it," said Claude, hopping off his horse as soon as they approached the White Cliff Inn. It was located at the top of one of the white cliffs of Dover, overlooking the channel. Dover was the closest point from England to France. Evelina had often been able to see the white cliffs of Dover from the shores of France on a clear day. The blue-green waters shone in the sun, and the vast sky was filled with swirling clouds.

"The view is breathtaking," said Evelina from atop the horse.

"Let me help you down." Felix reached up for her.

"Nay. You tend to the horses. I'll get her." Claude was

there instantly, reaching up and wrapping his hands around her waist and helping her dismount.

"Thank you," she said, staring out at the water. "Isn't this beautiful?"

Claude didn't even seem to notice the beauty all around them. "Stay here and look at the water if you want. I'll go inside and pick up the soul cakes. Then, we'll be off to get the rest of the supplies and be on our way back to Sandwich."

"But we just got here," protested Evelina, wanting to take some time to enjoy her surroundings.

"I have a job to do and need to get back to Rose's side." Claude was stubborn, and it would probably do no good to complain. He was in a hurry to get back to Rose and nothing she did was going to stop him.

"I'm hungry," complained Felix. "Something sure smells good coming from the inn."

"We'll eat when we get back to Briarbeck Castle and not before," growled Claude.

Claude left Evelina standing there, hurrying to the inn.

"What is the matter with him?" she asked Felix.

"I'm not sure," said Felix, tending to the horses. "I have never seen him act this way before. It is almost as if something is bothering him."

"Do you think it's me?" she asked.

"You?" Felix laughed, running his hand down the neck of the horse. "How could you bother anyone? You are a pure joy to be around. And a sight for sore eyes as well, I must add."

"You are too kind, Felix." She looked over at the inn. It was a small and quaint establishment made of wood with a clay-tiled roof. The aroma of food drifted on the breeze, making her mouth water. "I just wish I knew why Claude doesn't like me."

It wasn't but a few minutes later when Claude came out of the inn with a scowl on his face.

"Why the frown, my lord?" asked Felix.

"The innkeeper's wife says they are sold out of soul cakes. She needs to make more."

"How long will that take?" asked Evelina.

"She has to send one of her servants out to get more rosemary and lavender. She said it might take a few hours before they are ready."

"Good," said Felix. "That will give us time for an ale or two and mayhap a bowl of pottage."

"Nay. You'll take Evelina to town to get the rest of the things Lady Rose needs," said Claude. "I will wait here for the soul cakes."

"But the horses need to rest," complained Felix.

"The innkeeper has offered to lend you his horse and wagon. Just don't tarry." Claude looked out over the channel. His eyes narrowed. "There is a change in the wind. I have a feeling bad weather is on the way. I want to get back to Sandwich before it starts raining."

"Rain?" Evelina looked out over the sea. The sun was shining although there were clouds in the sky. "It is a beautiful day."

"Trust me. I know about storms. There is one coming,"

Claude grunted.

"Well, perhaps, we'd best be on our way then," Evelina told Felix.

* * *

While Evelina would have rather had Claude take her to town, she was thankful to be with Felix as well. He was much easier to talk to. Claude seemed very upset and fidgety today and a few minutes away from him might prove to be relaxing for all of them.

"Here's the clothier's shop." Felix stopped the wagon and tied the horse's reins to a post outside the shop. The town was small but, for the most part, in good condition. Several dirt streets were lined with buildings. Peasants, merchants and stray dogs filled the street.

There was a church at the far end of town. A group of men and a few women who looked like whores congregated outside the brewery. She noticed a cobbler's shop, a bakehouse, and a fishery on one side of the street. There was a furrier, butcher, and cordwainer's shop on the other. She thought about Lady Rose and Lady Isobel going shopping together for shoes. A part of her wished she was with them right now. She had never had any close friends, and those two seemed so happy.

"Let me help you," said Felix, guiding her from the cart to the wooden sidewalks.

"Thank you, Felix. I shouldn't be long." Evelina entered the shop to find a plump woman sitting in a chair, sewing.

A man who was most likely her husband was standing behind a counter.

"How can I help you?" asked the man.

"I am here to purchase . . . some things." She felt apprehensive asking the man for lady's undergarments. Their store was a small shop with a few long, suspended poles with hooks in them holding finished gowns. On the table were bolts of material and in the corner behind the counter was a bin with what looked like undergarments.

"Well, what is it you need?"

She looked over at the woman. "Lady Rose of Sandwich sent me to get . . . undergarments."

"Harold, I will help her." The woman put down her sewing and pushed her plump body from the chair. "Right this way." She led her over to the bin while her husband disappeared into the back room. "What size is Lady Rose?"

"She is nine months pregnant," answered Evelina.

The woman chuckled. "I don't have anything for pregnant women. Most garments are made to order, but I try to have a few things on hand. However, some of the things in this shop would fit you."

"I didn't think you'd really have anything to fit Lady Rose," said Evelina, realizing this was Rose's way of getting her alone with Claude. But Claude wasn't even near her. "Lady Rose did tell me to choose something for myself."

"A pretty young thing like you needs something like this." She plucked a shift and a drawstring pair of drawers from the pile and held them up. "By the way, my name is Beatrice."

"Thank you," said Evelina. "Those will be fine. I would like to look at your gowns as well."

"I think I have the perfect gown for you." The woman led her over to the pole and pulled down a simple gown made of wool. It was more for a commoner and did not look pretty at all.

"What else do you have?" asked Evelina, looking through the gowns. Each one was just as drab as the one before it. She was never going to catch Claude's eye wearing one of these.

"That's it, Missy."

Evelina noticed the gown the woman had been sewing when she walked in. It was made of purple velvet. "What about that gown?" asked Evelina.

"Oh, no. That is a gown for a noblewoman, not a commoner like you."

"Can I see it?" Evelina was tired of pretending to be a commoner. Perhaps if she dressed like a noblewoman, it would make it easier when she revealed her true identity to Claude. Then again, she wasn't at all sure that was a good idea. Everything confused her lately. Rose put thoughts in her head that Claude liked her, yet Evelina didn't see it. Perhaps, she should tell him she was a noble. Then, mayhap, he would treat her the way he treated Rose.

"It is one of my best works," said Beatrice excitedly, holding up the gown. "I even added lace on the bodice. Look at these tippets that trail all the way down to the ground."

Evelina ran her hand over the velvet, feeling empty and

sad inside. She couldn't go on much longer pretending to be someone she wasn't. She had thought by running away from her problems that she would be free. Instead, she had only created more. Would Rose and Claude hate her when she finally told them the truth? No one likes to be deceived. Even though she was a noble, she had deceived nobles. As far as she knew, she could be punished for that.

Perhaps, she should have stayed in France and married the evil Lord Onfroi of Grenoble after all. Now that she'd run away, her father was sure to be furious with her. And if Lord Onfroi was as evil as he was ugly, he was sure to raise a hand to her in punishment for trying to avoid him.

Evelina felt so alone with no one to confide in. Watching Claude and Rose had made her want the kind of friendship they had. Watching Rose and Toft made her feel as if she would never be in love the way they were.

"Evelina, are you almost finished?" Felix stuck his head inside the shop. "The sky is becoming very dark. I do believe Lord Claude was correct in saying a storm is brewing."

"I'll take it," said Evelina, pushing the gown back into the woman's hands.

"But I can't sell the gown to you," said the woman. "You can't wear the clothes of a noble."

Felix wandered inside and perused the gown that Beatrice held up. He whistled lowly. "That is one fine gown that any noblewoman would love. But I don't think it is going to fit Lady Rose until after the baby."

"Lady Rose will love it," said Evelina, hoping the shop

owner would think it was for a noble and sell it to her after all. "Wrap it up along with the undergarments," Evelina told Beatrice, pulling her coin pouch open and dipping her hand inside. "You wouldn't happen to have any rosewater, would you?"

"Nay, I don't," said the woman. "That is something only found in the baths of nobles."

"Please hurry," said Evelina, hearing the low rumble of thunder outside. Claude was sure to be in a foul mood since the storm was approaching and they had yet to return to the castle. In a matter of minutes, she was climbing onto the bench of the cart with the package in her hands.

Felix hopped up next to her, grabbing the reins and directing the horse back to the inn. No sooner had they left when the sky opened up in a downpour of rain. By the time they got back to the inn, they were soaked to the skin.

Claude stood at the door of the inn with his arms folded over his chest and a frown on his face.

"I'll take the horse and wagon to the stable and meet you inside," said Felix, helping Evelina from the cart.

In the pouring rain, she ran with the package, stopping at the door directly in front of Claude.

"What took you so long?" he growled. "I told you it was going to storm."

"I'm sorry," she said. "I had no idea we were gone that long. Please step aside so I can come in out of the rain."

"Why bother?" he asked. "As soon as the soul cakes are done we'll be leaving."

Felix ran up just then, coming to a halt right in front of Claude. He was dripping wet as well. "I can't wait to get in front of a warm fire with a tankard of ale," said Felix.

"Lord Claude says we shouldn't bother coming in out of the rain since we'll be leaving soon," Evelina explained.

"Leaving? In the midst of a storm?" Felix didn't like the sound of this, and neither did she.

As if on cue, a loud crash of thunder rumbled the earth. Two more flashes of lightning split the sky. Evelina was so cold her teeth started to chatter.

Claude looked out at the sky, and a dark shadow crossed his face. It seemed as if the storm upset him. "We need to get back to Lady Rose, but perhaps we can wait for a little while and see if the storm lets up. However, if we wait too long, we will be riding in the dark."

"I would rather ride in the dark than in the rain," said Evelina. "Please step aside and let us in to warm our bones. You need to stop being so unlikable."

CLAUDE FELT SHAKEN by the storm, as his memories of his time in Hastings Castle overwhelmed him still to this day. The last time he'd seen a storm like this, he'd almost died in the tower when his father's castle fell into the sea. He also didn't like the fact Evelina was so cold that her teeth were chattering.

He stepped aside and let them enter. "I've secured a table by the fire. I'll have the innkeeper send over some wine and ale and a hot meal."

"Thank you, my lord," said Felix, eagerly heading for the fire. Evelina started to follow him, but Claude's hand lashed out and grabbed her by the wrist.

"Are these the things for Lady Rose?" He took the package from her.

"I can hold on to them," she told him.

"You are dripping wet. I won't have Lady Rose's things ruined. Now go sit by the fire, and I'll have the innkeeper hold the package along with the soul cakes until we are ready to leave."

She didn't seem happy that he was offering to hold the package. But with another shiver, she nodded and followed Felix over to the fire.

Claude brought the package to the innkeeper. "Bertram, will you hold on to this package along with the soul cakes Josephine made until we are ready to leave?"

"Of course, my lord," said the man. "But by the looks of the storm brewing out there, I don't think you're going anywhere tonight. I have one room left if you'd like me to hold it for you before it's gone."

"Nay, we won't be staying."

"The girl with you is cold and wet and tired. If you take her anywhere in the rain, she is likely to get sick."

"She'll be fine." Claude handed the man the package. "Can you send over some wine and ale and a hot meal for my friends?"

"Do you mean your squire and the maidservant?" asked the man.

"Aye, that's who I mean." He dug into his pocket for

money to pay the innkeeper. Behind him, the door to the inn blew open, and a group of soldiers entered.

"It's getting worse out there," said one of the men.

"A tree blew over and nearly took our lives," said one of the other soldiers.

"No one better leave anytime tonight, or they'll be walking into the den of the devil," said another of the men. "Innkeeper, we need a room for the night."

"I've got only one room left," Bertram called out.

Claude glanced back to the fire where Evelina had her arms wrapped around her, trying to get warm. Her teeth chattered and her body shook. Water dripped from her hair and clothes. His squire sat next to her on the bench and underneath them was a large puddle.

Claude decided he couldn't take them out in the storm. He didn't want Evelina to get sick and die. Nay, he didn't want anything to happen to her because he cared about her. He was traveling with her, and it was his responsibility as a knight to protect her even if she was only a handmaid.

"Nay, you don't have any rooms available," Claude told him, handing Bertram a fistful of coins.

"My lord?" asked Bertram in confusion.

"I'll take the room for the night as well as a hot bath. Can I pay to stable my horses in the barn tonight as well?"

"You are welcome to the room as well as the barn for your horses, my lord. There is no charge since you are a noble."

"I might be a noble, but my friends aren't so I want you to take the money."

"Yes, my lord," said the man, greedily scooping up the coins and shoving them into his pocket. "Josephine," he called to his wife. "Have a bath sent upstairs for Lord Claude."

"It's not for me," he told the man, looking back at Evelina. "It's for the lady."

"The lady? You mean the handmaid?" asked the man. "My lord, where will you spend the night?"

"I'll sleep on the bench by the fire along with my squire," he told him.

"Pardon me for saying that I don't understand why you'd give up your room and bath for a mere maidservant, my lord."

"Nay, I don't suppose you'd understand. I can't say that I entirely understand either. All I know is that I am not going to let her shiver in wet clothes, being subjected to a bunch of drunken men all night. Now, do as I ask and do not question my actions again."

"Aye, my lord. At once."

Another crash of thunder shook the building, and Claude felt a knot forming in his stomach. This was going to be a very long night.

CHAPTER 11

Second in Command

*A*fter two cups of warm, spiced mead and a bowl of hot pottage, Evelina finally stopped shivering. Her clothes were still wet as well as her hair, but they had no chance of drying now that the inn was crowded with travelers all gathered around the fire.

Felix came in from outside, barely able to close the door since the winds were so strong. Tree branches and leaves flew through the air. Out the window, she saw the waves hitting the cliff and splashing up so high they were almost touching the inn.

Felix wove his way between the soldiers, peasants, and merchants that filled the inn. Finally, he made it over to where Evelina and Claude were sitting.

"My l-lord, the h-horses are s-secure in the b-barn for the night," he said, shivering worse than before Claude had sent him out in the storm.

"Good job, Squire." Claude pushed a bowl of pottage across the table. "Now have some food and warm up."

"T-thank you, my l-lord," he said, taking the bowl in two hands and gobbling down the food.

"I'll get you some spiced mead as soon as I can get the server's attention." Claude raised his hand in the air, but the place was so crowded that no one even saw him.

"Here, take the rest of my mead," said Evelina, handing Felix her cup.

"T-thank you," said Felix, drinking it down quickly. "The s-storm is bad out there, my lord. I d-don't think we should go anywhere yet."

"I agree," said Claude.

A fat, smelly man squeezed onto the bench next to Evelina, looking over and smiling at her, almost making her gag from the smell of his breath.

"My lord," said Josephine, making her way through the crowd. "Your bath and room are ready. It is room number one up the stairs and at the end of the hall."

"Thank you," said Claude, handing the woman a coin.

"I put your package as well as the soul cakes in the room," the innkeeper's wife explained. "With the crowd in here tonight, I didn't feel they would still be here come morning."

"Good idea," he told her. "I wouldn't want to disappoint Lady Rose."

Evelina was becoming quite disgusted hearing Claude talk about Lady Rose all the time. She also thought it was rude of him to secure a bath and room for himself while she and Felix were cold, wet, hungry and tired.

As soon as Josephine left, Claude stood up. "Come," he said.

"Where are we g-going?" asked Felix, looking up from his mead.

"I wasn't talking to you, Squire. I was talking to Evelina."

"Me?" She stood, only because she felt the fat man's hand wandering over to her leg and she was in a hurry to get away from him.

"I've had the innkeeper prepare a hot bath for you. You'll sleep in the room on the pallet tonight."

"What about m-me?" asked Felix.

"You'll stay here by the fire with me."

"It's c-crowded in here. C-can't we all share the room?"

"Nay. It wouldn't be proper. The room is only for Evelina."

"I d-don't think she'd m-mind," said Felix. "Would you, Evelina?"

"If you don't like the arrangements, you are welcome to stay in the barn tonight with the horses," Claude announced.

"N-nay, my lord. T-this is fine." Felix buried his nose in the cup of mead.

Evelina followed Claude up the stairs, glad to be away from the crowd, the drunks, and the noise. When they got to the end of the hall, he reached out and opened the door. She was about to enter the room when he stopped her.

"Let me make sure it is safe, first." He drew his sword and walked into the room.

Evelina thought he was overreacting. "I hardly think it is -" She stopped speaking when Claude pulled someone out of the shadows and held his blade to the person's throat. It was a young boy perhaps ten years of age. He had the package in his hands.

"You thought you'd steal from me, did you?" growled Claude.

Evelina stood there with her mouth hanging open.

"Please, don't kill me, my lord," begged the frightened boy.

Claude ripped the package from the boy's hands and threw it onto the pallet. "Why are you in here?"

"I am just a peasant," said the boy. "I work for the innkeeper and just finished bringing hot water for your bath." He pointed to an empty bucket on the floor.

"You were trying to steal my package," said Claude, using a voice that sounded very threatening. "You should know thieves stealing from nobles have their hands cut off."

"I wasn't stealing it," squeaked the boy. "I was just curious and wanted to know what was in it. Please don't cut off my hand, my lord."

"Sir Claude, please don't hurt the child," begged Evelina. "I believe he was just curious, that's all."

Claude sighed and lowered his blade. "Take your bucket and go," he told the boy. "Next time I catch you touching my belongings, you will find your hand next to you on the ground." He gave the boy a push, and he landed on the floor next to his bucket.

"Thank you, my lord," said the boy with wide eyes, still staring at Claude's sword. He picked up the bucket and ran out of the room.

"Thank you for not hurting the boy," said Evelina once the child had left the room.

"I wasn't going to hurt him. I just wanted to scare him." Claude slid his sword back into the scabbard. "If he doesn't learn his lesson now, someday another lord will cut off his hand or do something worse. A little fear as a child goes a long way."

Another rumble of thunder shook the building. Claude's body became rigid. He hurried over to the window and secured the shutter.

"You seem a little jumpy tonight," she told him, skimming her fingers over the surface of the bath water, sinking down to sit on the edge of the tub. The water felt hot and inviting. A fire burned in a small hearth at the other side of the room making it very cozy. The room was small and plain. The only other furnishings were a pallet lying directly on the floor and one chair.

"I don't like storms," he told her.

"Why not?"

"It doesn't matter. Now use the bath before it gets cold. I will be sitting outside the room to make sure nobody enters."

He grabbed the chair and headed for the door, but she

reached out and touched him. He stopped and looked over his shoulder.

"Thank you, Claude," she said, not using his title. Her eyes met his. She was alone with him and wanted to kiss him. Reaching up, she cupped his cheek in her hand. His eyes closed and he seemed to be holding his breath.

Evelina was taking a chance but she no longer cared. Claude's eyes were closed, and she used it to her advantage. Standing on her tiptoes, she reached up and gently kissed him on the lips.

His eyes snapped open. He almost looked frightened for a split second. Then his gaze became hooded and he leaned forward, his face coming closer to hers. And just when she thought he was going to return the kiss, he stopped.

"You are wasting hot water. Now use it before I throw you in the tub." With that, he turned and left the room carrying the chair.

CLAUDE CLOSED the door and sat on the chair, raking his hand through his hair in confusion. Evelina kissed him! And when she did, everything inside him came to life.

Damn, he liked it. The touch of her hand on his face and the gentle way she'd caressed his lips with hers about drove him out of his mind. He wanted to kiss her back, but he didn't. His feelings for her made him want to throw her down on the pallet, strip off her clothes and make love to her, but something made him stop.

She was only a handmaid. He shouldn't want her as much as he did. It was more than lust, and this is the part that scared him. He had a feeling deep down that somehow, some way they belonged together even if it didn't make any sense. Claude was a noble, and she was only a servant. Nay, he couldn't feel this way about her because love between a noble and a servant wasn't right. It was forbidden.

He also felt that by feeling this way he was somehow being disloyal to Rose. He understood that Rose was happily married to Toft, but a small part of him still held a flicker of hope that they would eventually end up together.

That was why he'd never married. Rose had broken his heart years ago. If he became vulnerable by falling in love with a woman and then she said she didn't want him, he wouldn't be able to face the pain. Being rejected by Rose was bad enough. He didn't need it to happen with another woman as well.

"God's eyes," he spat, hating himself for feeling this way. Rose didn't want him and made it very clear that they were only friends. So, why couldn't he let go?

He wanted Evelina, but the part of him that was still in love with Rose wouldn't let him feel the same way for Evelina. He leaned his head back against the wall and groaned. His body ached to have Evelina, but something was different than with past servants. He cared for her in a different way. She wasn't like any of the girls he'd bedded before. Something about her was special. Thinking about making love with her almost seemed sacred in his mind. When she looked into his eyes, he felt as if she could see into his very soul. She seemed to know him better than he knew himself. It wasn't just feelings of lust filling his emotions anymore. He cared about her as well.

However, she wasn't honest, and that bothered him. She never answered his questions directly or made it clear why she was in England in the first place or where she'd lived in France. He couldn't let down his guard and feel so strongly about a woman who was being deceitful. She might end up breaking his heart. He had to forget about Evelina. Nay, he had to forget about Rose. His head spun in confusion. The problem was he never wanted to forget either one of them, and that made him feel as if he were going mad.

* * *

EVELINA REMOVED her wet clothes and shoes and laid them on the floor in front of the fire, then slipped into the hot tub. Resting her head back against the side of the tub, she let out a satisfied sigh and closed her eyes. The water warmed her cold body. It felt comforting not to be in the tavern downstairs with a room full of smelly, drunken men.

Yes, she missed her life as a lady and decided it was time to make her identity known. She had a feeling Rose already knew she was a noble even though it was never mentioned. Evelina didn't think Rose or Isobel would blame her for taking on an alias trying to escape a betrothal and find love on her own. After all, both of them seemed to have found love with their husbands. Why couldn't it happen to her as well?

Even though she felt hurt that Claude hadn't returned her kiss, in a way it was probably for the best. She didn't want to deceive him anymore. It was time to tell him the truth. Evelina decided she would finish her bath and then tell Claude everything.

She hadn't meant to fall asleep. But she was so tired that when she awoke, the water in the tub was already cold. Climbing out of the tub, she dried herself with the towel that the servants left on the pallet. Finding a small vial next to it on the bed, she popped it open and took a sniff.

"Rosewater," she said with a smile, dabbing some behind her ears. The innkeeper must provide rosewater to the nobles who stayed there. She was about to see if her clothes were dry when she spotted the package on the bed.

Needing to look at the gown again, she decided to open the package. It was a beautiful gown, made for a lady. She had been wearing the clothes of a peasant for weeks now and longed to feel silk and velvet next to her skin once again.

With a quick glance back to the door, she checked to make sure no one was there. She would very quickly try on the gown to see if it fit. Hurriedly untying the twine, she opened the package and sighed when she laid eyes on the gown again.

Evelina decided to try on the undergarments as well. She quickly dressed, loving the feel of the clean, new clothes against her skin. The gown fit perfectly, making her feel pretty for the first time since she had left France.

Having no brush, she used her fingers to smooth and untangle her hair, quickly braiding it and throwing it over one shoulder. Now all she needed were the shoes Rose gave her, and she would feel like a lady once again. Happiness filled her being. She let out a squeal of delight.

The door banged open behind her. Evelina spun around to see Claude standing there with his sword in his hand, looking bewildered. His hair was mussed, and his eyes were half-closed. She figured he'd fallen asleep in the corridor.

"I heard you scream," he said with intensity to his words. His eyes made a quick sweep of the room. "Is everything all right? Did another thief enter the room?"

"I didn't scream. I squealed," she told him. His eyes settled on her, and he perused her from head to foot.

"What are you wearing?" he asked.

"It's the gown I bought. Do you like it?"

He took a moment to study her and then shook his head. "Take off Lady Rose's clothes, anon."

"It is not Lady Rose's gown," she explained. "It is mine."

"Yours? I don't understand."

"Come in and close the door, Claude."

"*Sir* Claude," he corrected her, stepping into the room and closing the door behind him.

"You see, *Sir* Claude," she started, stressing the word Sir. "Lady Rose gave me money to buy a gown for myself."

"You shouldn't be wearing that, Evie." He slid his sword back into the scabbard.

"What did you call me?" she asked, surprised by what she heard.

He cleared his throat and ran a hand over the back of his neck, looking down to the floor. "Evelina. That's what I said. Evelina."

"No, it wasn't," she said with a smile. "You called me Evie."

"Mayhap I did, but I was half-asleep. It won't happen again."

"Nay, I like it," she said, walking toward him slowly. "You can call me Evie if you want. Or better yet, you can call me . . . *Lady* Evelina."

CHAPTER 12

Second in Command

Claude heard what Evelina said, and shook his head. She had the nerve to lie about the gown, and now she was telling him to call her Lady. He didn't like the games she played. He stormed over to her and was about to reprimand her until the scent of fresh rosewater drifted up from her body, filling his senses and about driving him mad with desire.

"Don't play games with me, Evie," he told her, reaching out and lifting her chin with two fingers.

"I am not playing games," she told him. "Lady Rose told me to buy a gown for myself."

"Take it off. You can't wear the gown of a lady. Take it off now!"

Lightning flashed through the crack of the shutter and the rain pelted against it in the wind, making a loud hammering noise. Then the wind whistled through the shutter, blowing it open.

"God's eyes, enough with this storm." Claude hurried over and secured the shutter, feeling his body shake because of the storm. It was a storm just like this that frightened him as a child. It was the night his grandfather took his own life and Claude had almost lost his life, and so had his father. It brought back horrible memories of his father's castle falling into the sea. Even to this day, he couldn't get the terrifying images out of his mind.

"You're shaking," said Evelina, coming up behind him and placing her warm hand on his shoulder. He was faced toward the window and didn't turn around. "What's wrong, Claude? What has you so frightened? Is it the storm?"

It wasn't only the storm that frightened him. His desire for wanting a forbidden woman was scaring him as well. "I want you, Evelina," he spoke into the shutter rather than to turn and have to face her.

"What did you say?"

"You heard me. Don't ask me to repeat it."

"I want you, too, Claude."

He thought he'd heard her wrong, but when he turned around to face her, she was staring at him with want in her eyes.

"You asked me what scares me, well I'll tell you. You scare me."

"Me?" she giggled, filling the room with the sweet

sound of her voice. "I am not going to slap you again if you try to kiss me, if that is what you are thinking."

That was all he had to hear. He lifted her chin and leaned forward, kissing her full lips. He was already becoming heady. To him, she tasted like sweet ambrosia, the nectar of the gods, and he couldn't get his fill. This wasn't right. He had too many feelings for her that were more than lust, so he should just stop now. He envisioned them married with children, living in Stonebury Castle back in France, and shook his head to make the thought go away.

She tried to kiss him again, but he pulled back.

"Claude? What's the matter? Didn't you like the kiss?"

"Too much," he told her, letting out a sigh. "Evie, I can't do this right now."

"Why not?" Her brows dipped in disappointment. "Is it because you are still in love with Rose and refuse to accept that she is happily married to Toft? You need to let go of her, Claude. You are not children anymore. Rose is happy. Now, you need to be happy as well. If you don't release the past, you will never find happiness in the future. These thoughts will haunt you for the rest of your life."

Claude realized she was right. He had been holding on to the hope that someday he could be with Rose. But Rose told him they were just friends. Who was he to try to steal her happiness only to gain his? And would he even be happy if he did end up marrying Rose? Or would she consider him a friend and nothing more? He didn't want to waste his life mourning over what he could not have. He needed to love a woman – but one who was not forbidden to him.

"You are right," he told her. "I have been lying to myself, thinking I was still in love with Rose but, actually, I don't think I am."

"There is no shame in going after what you want," she told him. "Just be sure it is really what you want because you might end up getting it."

"I want you, Evelina," he told her again, pulling her into his embrace, and kissing the top of her head. He rubbed his cheek against her soft, silken hair and groaned. The scent of rosewater filled his senses, bringing his lust to life. "I want you, but I don't want you to play games with me anymore."

"I – I don't know what you mean."

He buried his nose against her neck, kissing her and using his tongue to taste her skin. She smelled fresh from her bath. It made him want to explore her body further.

"You do know what I mean. You've been lying to me, and I won't take it anymore."

"That's what I am trying to tell you, Claude. I don't want to lie to you anymore."

"I won't have you wearing the gown of a lady because it makes me want you even more."

"It does?" she asked.

"Remove it," he told her.

"I need to talk to you first, Claude."

"Either you remove it or I'll rip it off. But when I make love to you, I promise you it will be real and not pretend."

EVELINA'S JAW DROPPED. Did he just say he was going to make love to her? She should have tried harder to tell him she was a lady, but when he reached for her gown, she had to act quickly. "Please, don't rip the gown," she told him, liking it too much to see it ruined. "I will remove it, if that is what you want."

His eyes fastened to her as she slipped the gown down her shoulders and dropped it. It fell into a purple pool of velvet around her feet.

"My God, you are beautiful," he whispered, causing her to forget what she wanted to say. The firelight filled the room with an orange glow, and the sound of the snapping logs on the fire added romance to his seductive stare.

"Will you make love to me, Evie?"

Her body trembled at his request. She wanted this more than she had ever wanted anything in her entire life.

"Don't you want to know who I really am first?" she asked in a whisper, wanting to tell him but not wanting to ruin the moment.

"Nay. I don't want to talk about lies at this moment. I don't want to hear anything that will make me want to stop from giving you pleasure as you've never felt before."

It was a promise she wanted him to keep. The heat of desire spiraled through her. She wanted – needed to know how it felt to make love to Sir Claude Montague if it was the last thing she ever did in her life.

She nodded slowly. "I would like that, my lord."

His hands grabbed for his waist and, in one motion, he'd unfastened his weapon belt and laid it on the floor. Then he kicked off his shoes and removed his doublet and tunic. "Come to me, Evelina," he said, holding out his hand.

If there was a voice in her head warning her not to do this, she didn't hear it over the loud pounding of her heart reverberating in her ears. She flung herself into his embrace. Claude smothered her with hungry kisses, sweeping her off her feet.

She wrapped her legs around his waist, kissing him long and hard. This felt right. She was safe and protected in his strong arms. And when he slipped his tongue into her mouth, she felt a tingling between her thighs. His hardened form pressed up against her womanhood right through their clothes.

He fell to the pallet with her atop him, cradling her in his arms. Pushing her shift up and over her head, it left her bare breasts exposed. "You are even lovelier than I'd envisioned," he said, staring at her breasts. Bringing his mouth to one nipple, he used his tongue and lips to bring her to a rigid peak.

"Oh, Claude," she cried out, arching her back, feeling so wanton. Like a dirty little secret, acting this way only excited her, making her want him even more. His hands slid down her back, slipping under the top of her braies. His nimble fingers quickly untied them, and he pushed them down her legs, filling his hands with her rounded cheeks.

"God's eyes, Evie, you are perfect."

The sound of their heavy breathing filled the room. Evelina felt so hot she thought she was going to combust. Hurriedly slipping her hands around him, she managed to remove his braies as well.

The sight of his engorged manhood made her gasp. Shadows from the firelight danced on his body, and all she could think of was that he was the man she wanted in her life. He was the man she chose to marry and spend the rest of her life with from now on.

"Take me, Claude," she begged him. "Make me feel the pleasure you promised and do not stop until I cry out in ecstasy."

That turned his gentle touch to one of urgent, needed passion. He flipped her onto her back, bringing one leg around her, pressing his erection into her and making her cry out in need. As he leaned over, kissing her, his hand slid down her stomach ever so slowly. His fingers found and played with her nether hair and then he slipped one finger between her womanly folds.

"Oh, Claude," she moaned, lifting her hips to help his finger slide in and out guided by her liquid passion. Her breasts ached to have him suckle her again, so she pulled him to her and thrust her breast into his mouth.

His fingers moved faster as he suckled her nipple, bringing her closer and closer to reaching completion. And then he pulled back, spreading her legs apart, slipping in between them, watching her with hooded eyes.

"I don't want to hurt you."

"You could never hurt me, Claude. I am ready for you

so please don't deny me what I have waited for my entire life."

He slid his weapon of love into her, filling her completely like a sword slipping into a sheath. She heard him moan. When she looked at him, his eyes were closed, and his mouth was partially open. Evelina watched the rise and fall of her breasts as she tried to catch her breath.

Claude moved his hips slowly at first, sliding in and out teasingly, making her want to scream.

"No more teasing, Claude. I need you now. I am so close to my release."

His actions quickened. He thrust into her again and again, faster and faster as she lifted her hips to welcome him.

She couldn't get enough of him. She met him over and over in the throes of passion, feeling the vibrations of love bringing her to a precipice that she had never climbed before. Then Claude released his seed with a shout, and the excitement of it brought her to climax as well.

She had never felt so hot in her entire life. Neither had she ever felt so sated and satisfied as she did now.

Claude collapsed next to her on the pallet, holding her up against his chest and kissing her behind the ear.

"That was beyond words," she told him.

"You are the girl I have been waiting for my entire life," said Claude.

"Really?" Her heart beat faster. Mayhap, she had found a husband and wouldn't have to marry the wretched Lord Onfroi after all.

"I think I am falling in love with you, Evelina." His eyes closed partially, and he looked drained. "Why do I always fall in love with the wrong women?"

"Wrong?" She didn't understand. "What do you mean?"

"You know we can't be together forever because I am a noble and you – you are forbidden to me."

That was it. The time had come when she could finally tell him she was a lady and that they could be together after all. "It's not true," she said, staring at the ceiling. Claude's actions stilled, and his breathing slowed. "I tried to tell you before when I wore the gown, but you didn't give me a chance." He said nothing, and so she continued. "Claude, my real name is Lady Evelina du Pont. I am from the southern regions of France near Toulouse. My father is a count, and I ran away because I was betrothed to a man I didn't want to marry. But now that I found you, we can be married. I will talk to my father and convince him to break the betrothal. I love you, Claude and I want to be together forever. Don't you want that, too?"

He didn't answer. She started wondering if she'd divulged too much information too soon. Perhaps, she should have sprinkled in the truth little by little until he could accept it.

"Claude? Please don't be angry." Still, he didn't answer. "Claude?" She sat up to look at him just as he released a loud snore. He was sound asleep and hadn't heard a word she said.

Rain pounded down on the roof, and the winds continued to whistle through the cracks in the walls. The heat that had encompassed her suddenly left. Now, she felt chilled and frightened. What if Claude didn't want to marry her, even if he knew she was a lady? She hadn't considered that. If he turned her away, then she had doomed herself by giving her virginity to a man she couldn't have.

No man would want her if she weren't a virgin. And when her father found out that she'd acted like a strumpet instead of a lady, he would be so angry with her that he would probably put her in a nunnery for the rest of her life.

A tear dripped from her eye as thoughts filled her head that there was a life worse than marrying just for alliances. If she were in a convent, she would never feel love between her and a man ever again. Then again, if Claude turned her away, she wasn't sure she would ever want another man, because he was the one she loved.

CHAPTER 13

Second in Command

Claude woke the next morning to find Evelina lying next to him on the pallet. The fire had died, making the room cold. He slipped off the pallet without waking her and lit the fire. Then he came back to cover her with the blanket so she wouldn't be cold.

He stopped and stared when he noticed the bloodstain on the blanket. Clenching his jaw, he swore softly to himself.

God's eyes, she'd been a virgin! Why hadn't she told him? This thought upset him since he had meant to tell her this morning that what they did last night was a mistake. He sat down on the edge of the pallet, brushing back her hair and leaning forward to place a kiss on her forehead.

She made a noise that sounded like the purr of a kitten, turning and burying her cheek against the pillow

He felt awful for losing control last night. But his feelings for Evelina were strong. He couldn't remember exactly, but he thought he might have told her he was falling in love with her. Had she told him she loved him, too? He didn't think so.

What had he done? He fell in love with a merchant's daughter who liked to pretend she was someone she wasn't and told lies constantly. She'd even gone as far as telling him the gown was for her and that he should call her lady. Evelina was like a toxic drink to him. He had to have more, but when he did, it only shot pain through his heart that he never wanted to feel again.

Why had he been so careless? Now, he had only made things worse for both of them. He quickly dressed, and then peeked out the window to see that the storm had stopped. Claude never meant to be here this long. He was supposed to be with Rose and, instead, he was here doing things that this morning he wasn't proud of at all.

He'd taken a young woman's virginity, and now he was going to have to break her heart. But what did it matter since his heart was broken, too?

Claude picked up one of the travel bags and started wrapping soul cakes in Evelina's peasant gown, shoving them into the pack.

"My lord, my lord," came Felix's voice as he pounded on the door.

Claude hurried over and opened the door, scowling at his squire. "What is wrong with you, making so much noise so early in the morning?" He noticed a guard from

Briarbeck Castle standing at Felix's side. "What is it?" he asked. "What's the matter?"

"It's Lady Rose, my lord," said Felix.

"Rose?" His heart almost stopped. "Bid the devil, don't tell me something has happened to her."

"It's her baby," said the guard. "It started last night in the storm."

"The baby?" Claude's body stiffened. "What is it? Has the baby been born?"

"Not yet," said the guard. "Lady Rose is having a hard time. The baby does not seem to want to come out. She sent me to find you. You need to return anon. My lord, I am afraid Lady Rose might not make it through this, and neither will her baby."

"Damn you," spat Claude, dropping the travel bag and gripping the man by the front of his tunic. "Why didn't you get here faster?"

"The storm was too dangerous, my lord," said the guard. "As it is, I rode in the rain to get here this morning. I had to wait until sunup because too many roads are washed away. I had to find an alternate route."

"Let's go," said Claude, rushing back into the room to grab his weapon belt and fastening it around his waist. He scooped up the travel bag and stepped out into the corridor. "We have no time to waste."

"Claude?" Evelina peeked around the door with sleepy eyes, clutching the blanket around her bare body. "What is happening?"

"Damn," he spat, forgetting momentarily all about her.

He had no time to wait for her to dress, and riding double was only going to slow them down. "Felix, you'll wait for Evelina, and bring her back to the castle with you."

"Are you leaving?" asked Evelina. "I don't understand."

"It's Rose," said Claude, taking one last look at Evelina. He wished things were different and wanted nothing more than to go back to bed and hold her tightly in his arms.

"It's Rose?" she asked, looking at each of the men in turn.

"She needs me," said Claude. "I should have been with her, but I was here instead. Now, because of my foolishness, the woman that means everything in the world to me might die!" He hurried away with the guard, only hoping he could make it back to Rose before it was too late.

* * *

EVELINA PACKED the soul cakes into a travel bag and went to get her old clothes by the fire, only finding the shoes. She smiled at the shoes Rose had given her, running a hand over the soft, embroidered slippers. Then she picked up the purple gown and pulled it over her head. It had felt wonderful being a lady for the night, although she couldn't say she wasn't embarrassed at the way she'd conducted herself around Claude.

But making love to Claude felt right, even if she had given her virginity to a man that might not marry her after all. By the way he said Rose was the woman who meant everything in the world to him, it sounded like he was still in love with her after all. She thought things would be different after last night and that he'd care for her the way he cared for Rose. But this morning, he almost seemed to forget she was even there.

She hurriedly shoved the rest of her things into the travel bag, worried about the fate of Rose as well. It bothered her how Claude took off in a hurry to be at Rose's side, not even taking a moment to say good morning to her. Was she being selfish and petty in such a time of need? Mayhap so, she wasn't sure.

Had their coupling meant nothing to him? He told her he was falling in love with her, but he certainly didn't act like it this morning.

"Evelina?" Felix knocked and then stuck his head in through the partially open door.

"Felix, I am ready," she told him. "Let's hurry to help Rose."

"I'm afraid we can't leave yet," he told her.

"Can't leave? Why not? Rose is in trouble."

"I understand. But unfortunately, the horse we are using has thrown a shoe."

"Well, get a blacksmith, quickly."

"The blacksmith is in town, so we'll have to walk with the horse until we get there."

"Walk?" She looked down to her velvet gown and soft slippers. "Then I will have to change into my other clothes." She looked through the travel bag but couldn't find them. "Where are they?"

"Perhaps they are in the travel bag I saw Lord Claude take with him."

"Well, then I will have to wear my good clothes, but I am afraid they will get ruined."

"You look very pretty today," said Felix. "Isn't that the gown of a lady?"

"Aye, it is," she told him. "I am wearing it because I am a lady, pretending to be a handmaid."

"You are?" Felix's eyes opened wide in surprise.

"My name is Lady Evelina du Pont from France. My father is a count."

"By the rood," said Felix, holding on to the doorframe for support. "Does Sir Claude know this?"

"I tried to tell him, but I don't think he understood. Or at least, he didn't believe me."

"Why are you pretending to be a handmaid?" he asked.

"I will tell you all about it on the long walk to town." She picked up the travel bag and slung it over her shoulder.

"Nay, let me carry that, my lady," said Felix, taking the bag from her. She smiled. Felix accepted the news easily. Now, if only Claude would feel the same way, it would help. However, somehow, she thought he would have an entirely different reaction.

CHAPTER 14

Second in Command

Riding like the devil was on his heels, Claude made it back to Briarbeck Castle in good time. Even with the flooded roads and alternate route, he didn't let it deter him from getting to Rose's side.

He rode into the courtyard, jumping off the horse and tossing the reins to a stable boy. Then he grabbed the travel bag with the soul cakes in it and ran toward the keep. His mother was there to greet him just outside the great hall. She had a discontented look on her face, so he knew the news was not going to be good.

"How is Rose?" he asked, giving his mother a quick hug and peck on the cheek.

"Not good, Claude. She is having a very difficult time with the birth of the baby. It is too big and does not want to be born. The midwife said she has lost a lot of blood.

The longer it takes, the less chance of Rose or the baby surviving."

"Nay," shouted Claude, "I will not let Rose or the baby die. It is my responsibility to protect her. This is all my fault since I was not here." He rushed down the corridor toward Rose's chamber with his mother right behind him.

"This is nobody's fault, Claude, so don't blame yourself. It is just an act of nature."

"I won't let her die!" he said, bursting into her room and stopping short when he saw Rose lying on the bed looking whiter than a ghost. Rose's stepmother, Isobel, was with her as well as the midwife and several servants.

"Claude!" Rose called out, trying to raise her hand but dropping it to the bed since she was so weak. "You came."

"Of course, I did." He hurried to the bed, putting down the travel bag and taking both of Rose's hands in his. "I am here to protect you and the baby. If I have to reach in there myself and pull the stubborn thing out, I swear, I'll do it."

Rose smiled slightly. A peaceful look washed over her face. "Now that you are here, I can die in peace. I only wish Toft and my father were here as well."

"You are not going to die, and neither is the baby," Claude told her. "I promise you that."

"I sent men out in the storm last night to get a message to yer faither and Toft as well as Claude," Isobel told them. "Hopefully, they will be here soon."

A vein in Claude's jaw ticked in aggravation upon hearing this. So, the guard had lied about not being able to leave until morning. He had probably stayed holed up in a tavern all night long. Claude was so tired of being lied to.

"I brought you soul cakes to make you feel better," said Claude, ripping open the travel bag and grabbing Evelina's coarse, woolen gown that he'd wrapped them in. "Here," he said holding out one of the round cakes that fit in the palm of his hand and was very similar to a bun.

"Claude," said Rose, reaching out and laying her cold hand on his. She feigned a smile. "I didn't really want soul cakes. I only said that to give you time alone with Evelina."

"What?" he asked, pulling back the cake.

"Where is Evelina? I need her here as well."

"She is coming later with Felix."

"Why didn't she come back with you? Is everything all right between the two of you?"

"Shh, Rose, don't use your energy to speak. She will be here soon."

Rose cried out with pain, sending a shiver up Claude's spine.

"Breathe," commanded the midwife, looking under the sheet and between Rose's legs. Then the woman looked up at Isobel and shook her head.

"What's wrong?" asked Claude. "Someone tell me."

"*Claude Jean tu dois être tranquille. Vous allez seulement effrayer Rose.*" His mother told him in French to be quiet and still so he wouldn't scare Rose. Then she told him if he didn't behave he would have to leave the room.

"I am not going anywhere," Claude told her, taking hold of Rose's hand. "You will be fine, Rose. Just be strong."

"I don't know if I can do it, Claude. I think I am going to die giving birth, just like my mother. It is my biggest fear."

Claude remembered what Evelina had told him last night. He needed to tell Rose the same thing. "If you don't let go of the past, you will never find happiness in the future," he told her. "Don't think about what happened before, think about what is yet to come. You and Toft are going to be parents, and I envy you, Rose. You have a wonderful life and need to know it."

"Oh, Claude, you are right." Rose's eyes began to close. "You need to marry Evelina because you two are meant to be together."

"Hush, don't speak," he told her.

"Nay. I will say this if it is the last thing I ever say. Claude, you are my best friend, but you are blind when it comes to love."

"What do you mean, Rose?"

"Don't let her slip away. Evelina loves you, and I know you have feelings for her, too."

"She's a handmaid. I'm a knight."

"Where love is concerned, status shouldn't matter." Rose had another contraction and cried out in pain.

"You need to push, my lady," said the midwife. "Push, push."

"I can't. I am too tired and weak. I want my father. I want Toft." Tears flowed from her eyes.

Claude felt so helpless that it caused him great pain as well. "I will see if they've returned yet," said Claude, jumping up and heading out the door. His mother followed.

"Claude Jean," she said, causing him to stop and turn around. "The baby hasn't moved for some time now. The midwife thinks it is going to be stillborn."

"Nay. That will break Rose's heart." Claude paced back and forth.

"I heard what Rose told you about Evelina. Do you have feelings for this girl?"

"Aye. Nay. I don't know." He dragged a hand through his hair in frustration. "I am confused, Mother. I think I am in love with Evelina, but I know a marriage between us would be forbidden."

"There are a lot of things forbidden in this lifetime, but not unless we want them to be. Now go, look for Conlin and Toft. I need to get back to comfort Rose. I only hope she will not die because that would be the worst thing for all of us."

Claude made his way out to the courtyard, so upset he couldn't think straight. He didn't see Toft or Conlin, but Felix rode through the gate with Evelina holding on to the back of him.

"Felix. Evelina." He ran over to join them, lifting Evelina from the horse, looking at her oddly and shaking his head. Her new gown and shoes were covered in mud. "What happened to you?" he asked.

"We had to take a few backwoods roads to get here, and they were not in the best condition," said his squire. "Not to mention, when the horse got spooked, Evelina fell off in a puddle of mud."

"Are you all right?" he asked her.

"Never mind me, how is Rose?" Evelina wiped her dirt-streaked face with the back of her hand.

"It isn't looking good. Rose is weak and has lost a lot of blood. The baby hasn't emerged or even moved in quite some time now. She has been asking for her husband and father, but they have yet to return."

"I need to go to her," said Evelina very determined. "I will not let her or her baby die." She started to hurry toward the keep, but Claude pulled her to him and kissed her passionately on the mouth.

"Uh, I think I had better tend to the horse," said Felix, slinking away.

"What was that for?" she asked him, looking up with bright eyes.

"I wanted you to know that I love you, Evelina." He used his thumb to brush the dirt off her cheek.

"I love you, too, Claude. I am not sorry for what happened between us last night."

"Neither am I." He knelt on the cobblestones and took her hands in his.

"Claude, get up. What are you doing?"

"Marry me, Evie. I want you to be my wife."

"What?" That seemed to surprise her. "You would ask me to marry you even though you said a marriage between two people of different statuses is forbidden?"

"Rose and my mother helped me to realize that I've

been acting like a fool. You helped me to see that I have been stuck in the past and therefore blind to the future. What is your answer, Evie? Will you marry me?"

EVELINA COULDN'T BELIEVE Claude was down on one knee in the middle of the courtyard asking her to marry him. Her heart soared with joy but, at the same time, she felt frightened. She'd yet to tell Claude who she really was. She couldn't tell him yes until she got out of the other betrothal with Lord Onfroi. Why was everything so complicated?

"My lord," said a female servant, running from the keep. "Lady Rose is asking for her father and husband. She is slipping in and out of consciousness. Lady Isobel sent me to ask if you have seen her husband arrive."

"Claude," said Evelina. "I am honored by your proposal, but before I give you my answer, we need to talk. It will have to wait because, right now, Lady Rose's life is at stake."

"Of course," he said, getting to his feet. "I apologize, I am not thinking clearly."

"Why don't you ride to the docks and see if any ships have arrived with Lord Conlin and Sir Toft?" she suggested, seeing that the events of the past few days weighed heavy on Claude's mind.

"I need to be with Lady Rose," he protested.

"I will be there, and so will your mother and Lady Isobel. There is nothing you can do for Lady Rose but find her father and husband. It is her request."

"Then I will go anon. Squire," he called out. "Fetch me a horse. We are riding to the docks. When we return, I swear we will have Baron Conlin and Sir Toft with us. This is Lady Rose's request, and I will not let her down."

Evelina was glad Claude left for the docks because she couldn't give him an answer before having a long talk with him. But right now, she needed to be with Rose. If Rose died, there would be a lot of people, especially Claude, who would never be the same again.

She hurried into Rose's chamber, stopping at the door when she saw her nearly lifeless body on the bed. Rose cried and writhed in pain.

"Lady Rose. I am here." Evelina hurried forward, but the midwife stopped her.

"You are filthy. Do not come near Lady Rose like that," warned the woman.

"Nay, I want her here." Rose lifted her hand and reached into the air. Evelina ran to her and cradled her head in her arms, trying not to get her dirty.

"Evelina - your gown," said Rose, looking up with tearstained cheeks.

"I bought the gown of a lady, just like you suggested."

"I don't think that dirty gown will attract any man, let alone Claude."

"It wasn't dirty when I got it." Evelina forced a smile, hoping it would help ease Rose's pain. "How are you, Rose?"

"I am dying," she responded.

"You are not dying," Celestine told her, coming to the

other side of the bed. "I had a vision of you and Toft with your healthy baby. My visions are never wrong."

"I hope you're right," said Rose, screaming out in pain once again. "I can't do this," she cried. "I am finished."

The women all looked at one another, and the midwife shook her head.

"Do not talk that way," scolded Evelina, trying not to let her fear show in her voice. "Do you want the last thing that Toft remembers of you is that you gave up? He loves you, Rose. Don't let him down. If you won't keep trying for yourself or for the baby, then do it for your husband."

"I will," said Rose. "I can't let Toft down. And if I die, my father will blame himself for the rest of his life because he wasn't here, just like he wasn't here when my mother died."

"Don't do that to him, Rose," Evelina urged her. "You are stronger than this. Now gather up that strength and all the love you have for Toft and for your father, and help your baby be born."

"Her daughter," said Celestine. "I saw in my vision that she is going to have a girl."

"Evelina, I'm scared," Rose cried out.

Isobel rushed over and grabbed one of Rose's hands while Evelina took the other.

"Ye can do this, Rose," Isobel assured her. "Ye have always been strong and a survivor. Now listen to Evelina, and do no' let yer faither or yer husband down."

"I will. I can do this," said Rose, gathering her composure.

"Try again," said the midwife. "Take a deep breath and this time push with all your might."

"Your daughter needs your help to come into this world," said Evelina. "You have all the strength you need, Rose, because we are all here to help you."

Rose gripped Isobel's and Evelina's hands tightly and screamed out as she pushed so hard that her face turned red and her body shook.

"It moved. The baby moved! I see her face," exclaimed the midwife. "Do it again, Rose. Push harder."

"One more push and it will all be over," Evelina told her, not sure if it was true, but wanting to give Rose hope.

"I will do it," said Rose. "I can do it," she said with determination in her eyes. Rose was a small girl like Evelina, but her will and determination were bigger than even the strongest warrior. One more push and Rose screamed louder than before. And then, as if it were a miracle, Evelina heard the sound of a crying baby.

"You did it," exclaimed Evelina, seeing the midwife hold up one of the biggest newborns she had ever seen. "Your baby is born. I knew you could do it."

"I couldn't have done it without you," Rose told her, holding out her arms for her baby. The midwife cleaned it up quickly and laid it on top of Rose's chest.

"She's beautiful," said Evelina, wishing that someday she would have a child of her own. She wanted to marry Claude more than anything and hoped it could be so.

* * *

NOT A HALF-HOUR LATER, Toft, Conlin, and Claude rushed into the bedchamber.

"Rose," called out Toft, running to her side. "I am here, Rose." He stopped in his tracks when he laid eyes on the baby. "Y-you had the baby?"

"I did," said Rose with a smile. "Our daughter is alive and healthy. So am I. We have Evelina to thank for talking me through this."

"Rose, thank God you are all right," said Conlin, rushing to the bedside to be with his daughter. "When we got the message, we came right away. King Edward sent us home, and he sends his best wishes as well."

"Our daughter is beautiful and so are you, Rose." Toft scooted onto the bed next to her and put his arm around his wife. "What will we name her?"

"I felt like Daniel in the lion's den birthing her," said Rose with a smile. "Mayhap, we should name her Daniela."

"I like that," said Toft. "Daniela, it is."

"Rose, I am so glad you and the baby made it through this." Claude, who was standing silently and watching, stepped forward and kissed Rose on the head.

"Thank you, Claude, for staying in England with me. That meant the world to me."

"I would do anything for you and your baby." Claude reached out and ran a finger lightly over the baby's head. "After all, what are good friends for?"

"Thank you, Claude," said Toft with a nod of his head. "If anything had happened to Rose, I don't know how I would go on without her."

"Claude, I was hoping we could talk now," said Evelina softly.

For the first time, Claude turned to look at her. But to her surprise, he was not smiling.

"I think a talk is in order. But first, someone is waiting in the great hall to see you."

"Me?" she asked, not knowing what he meant.

"When I went down to the docks, I found Lord Conlin and Sir Toft, but they were not the only ones I found."

"Who did you find, Claude? I don't understand."

"There was a ship from France that had just docked," Claude explained. "To my surprise, two men approached me and asked if I knew a girl named Evelina."

"They did?" It was evident where this was leading, and it wasn't good.

"Evelina, or should I say, Lady Evelina, your father, Count du Pont is waiting for you in the great hall along with Lord Onfroi Faucheux – your betrothed."

CHAPTER 15

Second in Command

*C*laude left Rose's room and headed down the corridor, wanting to get as far away from Evelina as possible.

"Claude, please wait," Evelina called out, running after him. "I need to talk to you."

"It's a little too late for that," he growled, having been devastated to hear that Evelina was not only a lady pretending to be a servant, but also already betrothed to someone else. First, he'd had his heart broken by Rose. And then when he decided to open his heart to a woman he thought he loved, the door was slammed in his face, and a dagger pushed through his heart once again.

"Claude, please." Evelina reached out and grabbed his arm and he spun around on his heel, feeling angrier than hell.

"Why, Lady Evelina?" he asked. "So you can make a fool

of me once again? Why didn't you tell me who you were and that you were already promised to another man before we made love?"

"I tried to, but you didn't give me a chance."

"You had more than enough chances, but yet you continued to lie. I gave my heart to you, but you thrust a dagger right through it."

"I didn't mean to hurt you, Claude." Tears formed in her eyes.

"I knew I shouldn't have trusted you, but I let down my guard. That is what I get for making the mistake of falling in love."

"I love you, Claude."

"God's eyes, Evelina, stop already." He threw his hands up into the air. "I bent down on one knee in front of everyone and asked you to marry me although I thought you were only a merchant's daughter pretending to be a maidservant."

"I wanted to tell you, but Rose was dying. Please, you need to believe me that I never meant to make a fool of you."

He ignored her pleas and shook his head. His top lip curled up as he said his next words. "I took your innocence. Now, I might go to war over it. I am an honorable man and would never take another man's bride."

"You don't understand. I don't want to marry Lord Onfroi. He is evil and hurts women. I love you and want to marry you."

"We can't be married, Evelina. You are betrothed to another man. So, once again, you are forbidden to me."

"I'll ask my father to break the betrothal. I'll tell him it is you I love and no one else."

"I am disappointed in you," he told her. "I truly loved you, and now you've broken my heart."

"I didn't break your heart. Everything I said about loving you is true."

"How can I believe you? You have done nothing but lie to me since the day I met you. Even if we did marry, how could I trust that you wouldn't tire of me and go looking for another husband instead?"

"I would never do that, Claude." The tears ran down her cheeks. He longed to reach out and comfort her and wipe her tears away, but he couldn't. She belonged to another man. He had no right to love her. Once again, he had fallen into a trap and found himself in a situation with a forbidden love.

"Go to your betrothed, Evelina. You belong to him, not me." Claude turned and quit the keep, heading for the stable to take a ride alone to clear his very confused mind.

"Evelina," said Celestine, coming up to her side. "I saw Claude leave. Is anything wrong?"

"It is," she told Claude's mother. "I have done something very foolish. I am afraid I have hurt Claude deeply. I am a lady, but I didn't tell him. I left France because I didn't want to be betrothed to a man my father chose."

"You need to talk to Claude."

"I did. He doesn't want to listen. He thinks I purposely betrayed him just to hurt him, but I didn't. I love him. He asked me to marry him earlier, but now he wants nothing to do with me."

"Claude asked you to marry him?" Celestine seemed surprised and pleased.

"I never even had a chance to give him my answer. Now it is too late. Oh, Lady Celestine, what am I going to do?"

"The first thing you need to do is to confront your father and your betrothed."

"I'm frightened," said Evelina.

"We'll go with ye to talk to them." Lady Isobel and Lord Conlin walked hand in hand down the corridor toward her.

"Come, Lady Evelina," said Celestine. "Face your fears the way you taught Rose and Claude to face theirs. Everything will work out in the end."

"Did you have a vision?" asked Evelina hopefully.

"I did not. However, I know what a strong woman you are and that you would never give up on love and a man you believed in, would you?"

"Nay, I won't give up on Claude," said Evelina. Holding her head high, she entered the great hall behind Lady Isobel and Lord Conlin.

"Evelina, thank God I found you." Her father, the Count of Tarbes, rushed forward with Lord Onfroi right behind him.

"Father," she said, swallowing forcefully, wishing

Claude were at her side to help her through this. "How did you find me?"

"The mercenary returned and told us that you paid him to escort you to England," said Onfroi. "Why in God's name would you do that?"

"Aye," said her father. "And why are you wearing a gown covered in mud?"

"Augustin told us you were posing as a servant," added Onfroi. "Are you daft? I should take you across my knee for even playing such a game."

Evelina shuddered, knowing Lord Onfroi would have no qualms with hitting her.

"Pack your things, Daughter, we are heading back to France at once," said the count.

"Count du Pont," said Conlin, stepping forward. "It is a shame you have to leave so soon. I would like to show you the docks and, perhaps, talk about a trade since you've come all the way from France."

"What kind of trade?" Onfroi broke in. "You are a Baron of the Cinque Ports, aren't you?"

"I am," said Conlin. "And who would you be?"

"I am Lord Onfroi Faucheux of Grenoble. I am Lady Evelina's betrothed."

"Ah, I see," said Conlin. "So, your betrothal to Lady Evelina is an alliance."

"Of course, it is," the man snapped. "Why else would I be marrying her? Look at her in that bedraggled gown with dirt from head to foot. When she's my wife, she will never walk around looking like that."

"Some men marry for love," Conlin told him. "It isn't always about money or what you can gain."

"That's nonsense," he spat.

"We married for love," Isobel spoke up.

"So did my daughter," said Conlin.

"What is this all about?" asked the count. "Why are you even saying this?"

"Father, I am in love with another man. I cannot marry Lord Onfroi," Evelina blurted out.

"You're what?" gasped her father.

Evelina continued. "His name is Sir Claude Jean Montague. He is a French, just like us."

"He is?" asked the count. "What holdings does he have?"

"I don't know," said Evelina, "but neither do I care. I would marry him even if he were penniless because I fell in love with him."

"She's lying," spat Onfroi. "Besides, she is already betrothed to me. The deal has been made."

"Hold on, Onfroi." The count held up his hand. "Where is this Sir Claude Montague? I would like to meet him."

"I - I don't know where he went," said Evelina. "He became angry when he found out I hadn't told him the truth and he left me."

"There," said Onfroi with a satisfied smirk. "The man doesn't want her anyway, so I see no need to continue this conversation. Come, Evelina, we are going back to France to be married anon." He grabbed her by the arm, but she pulled away.

"Nay! I don't want to marry you."

"You'll not talk back to me and get away with it." His fist shot out to hit her. Lord Conlin's body blocked her, and he grasped the man's hand and squeezed.

"We don't hit women at Castle Briarbeck," Conlin said through gritted teeth. "Show some respect, for God's sake, and stop acting like an ass."

"I'll show you who is acting like an ass." Onfroi pulled out of his grip and went for his sword, but the tip of another sword pressed up against his throat and stopped him.

"You try to touch her again, and I'll have your head no matter if you are her betrothed or not," said Claude, coming to her rescue.

"Claude," cried Evelina, so happy to see him.

"I heard everything, Evie, and I believe you love me. I don't want to see you married to a cur like this."

"Lower your sword, Sir Knight," commanded the count.

Claude glanced over to Evelina, and she nodded slightly. Slowly, Claude lowered his sword and backed away.

"Are you Sir Claude Montague who my daughter says she wants to marry?" asked the man.

"I am." Claude kept his mouth in a firm line and nodded his head as he shoved his sword back into the sheath.

"You are very brave to stand up to Lord Onfroi when you know he is betrothed to my daughter."

"I fear nothing when I am protecting those I love," Claude answered.

"There is that word again. Love," said the count, chuckling and nodding his gray head. "When Evelina's mother was alive, she believed in marrying for love as well, although I always believed in marrying for alliances."

"What are you saying, my lord?" asked Claude.

"I am saying I like you, Sir Montague. I didn't know until today that Lord Onfroi intended on hurting my daughter."

"She needs to be kept in line," snarled Onfroi. "A good beating is what she needs, and I'll be the one to give it to her. After today, she will never run off or lie to us again."

"After today, you will need to find a new wife," said the count. "I am sorry, Lord Onfroi but I cannot let you marry my daughter."

"We made an alliance," shouted Onfroi. "Do you want to go to war with me over this?"

"If I have to fight you to protect my daughter, then I will do it. Now, I suggest you leave the castle immediately because the longer you stay here, the more you are making me want to run my blade through you myself."

"You'll pay for this, du Pont. You won't get away with crossing me." Onfroi left the great hall, making Evelina let out a sigh of relief.

"Claude, can you ever forgive me?" asked Evelina. "I am sorry for everything. I promise that if you can forgive me for my mistakes, I will never make them again."

"You hurt me deeply," Claude admitted. "But when I left here in anger, I realized that I was only hurting myself."

"What do you mean?" asked Evelina.

"You were the one who taught me that I have to let go

of the past or I will never be able to enjoy the future. Well, I want to look forward to the future, but only if you are a part of it as my wife." Claude got down on one knee again and took Evelina's hands in his. "Will you marry me, Lady Evelina? I love you and want you to be my wife."

Evelina wanted this more than anything, but she needed her father to agree to it first. She realized she should never have gone against him without talking to him and explaining how she felt. Knowing now that her mother believed in marrying for love, she could see if she had tried harder to talk with her father they might have been able to come to a decision that benefited both of them. She looked up at her father, feeling her heart beating rapidly in her chest, waiting for his permission.

"Go on," said the count with a chuckle. "I wouldn't want to get in the way of a love like that."

"I will," said Evelina, feeling as if her dreams had come true. "I will marry you, Claude Montague, and I am honored to be your wife."

CHAPTER 16

Second in Command

THREE DAYS LATER

Claude stood atop the cliff at Hastings, having just said his vows and marrying Evelina. She looked beautiful wearing the purple velvet gown that was now clean and fit for a princess. A circlet of freshly picked flowers crowned her head. They left the priest and crowd of people at the foot of the cliff because Claude wanted to bring Evelina up to the ruins of Castle Hastings. It was such a big part of his past.

Claude had chosen to be married in Hastings because it was once his father's demesne and where Claude's life changed forever.

The count had stayed in England for the wedding, and Lord Onfroi hadn't been seen again since he was sent away. Everyone was there to celebrate, including the Barons of the Cinque Ports and their families, and even Rose and Toft and their new baby, Daniela.

"I can't believe we're married," said Evelina, glancing down at the ring on her finger. Claude had given her a ring that was his late grandmother's, on his father's side. His grandfather insisted Claude take it for good luck.

"I can't believe it either," he said, looking up to the ruins where half of the castle still clung to the cliff hanging over the silted-up harbor far below.

"Claude, why are we here?" asked Evelina, looking over at the ruins. "This doesn't seem like the best place for a wedding."

"I think it is a perfect place," he told her, wrapping his arms around her, pulling her back against his chest. "This was once my father's castle. It was his pride and joy. There was a bad storm one night, and he lost almost everything – except his family and those he loved."

"Go on," she said, urging him to continue.

"See that broken tower," he told her, pointing up to the castle.

"I do."

"That is where I almost died."

"Oh, Claude, that is horrible."

"Nay, not really. My father saved my life that day. Then, my mother and I saved his life in return. It was also where my grandfather took his own life."

"I still don't understand why you would want to come here to get married."

"It wasn't the act, but the love I felt that day that made me want to return. I learned a lot at the young age of five and ten years. I learned to forgive, and I learned that love is stronger than any blade. It is all that really matters."

"That is beautiful, Claude. I think I understand now."

"There is more," said Claude. "I realized that wanting to return here was only clinging to the past. And since I am looking forward to the future, I want to leave the bad memories behind and only bring with me the good feelings from now on."

"That is wonderful, Claude. I am happy for you. Now, you need to show you are leaving your past behind by throwing something into the sea."

"Like what?" he asked.

"Not me," she said, causing both of them to laugh. "Take this," she said, removing her crown of flowers and handing it to him. "By throwing it into the sea, you will be releasing everything from the past that has been holding you back. The flowers symbolize life. As they float in the water, they will either wash out to sea or back to shore, but it doesn't matter. They symbolize new life, new growth and new love."

"I love you," said Claude, taking the crown, stepping forward and tossing it over the edge of the cliff and into the sea. "There," he said, taking her hand. "Now we can celebrate with our loved ones and start our new life without anything holding us back."

They ran happily down the hill and didn't stop until they met with the others.

"Claude," said his father, John, coming up to him with a look of concern on his face. "What were you throwing into the sea?"

"Don't worry, Father, I was just getting rid of some things I didn't need any longer."

"Aye, and nature did that for your father, getting rid of that big ol' castle that he used to brag about all the time," said Lord Nicholas Vaughn with a chuckle.

"Easy, Nicholas," John warned him. "If you keep that up I am going to have to remind everyone that you still are living in a manor house while I have a new castle just about built in Winchelsea."

"Don't worry, Nicholas, I'll lend you one of my castles if you need it," said Lord Conlin -.

"Conlin, our second castle is in Scotland," said Isobel. "Nicholas and Muriel and their children are happy in New Romney."

"That's right," said Nicholas' wife, Muriel, who used to be a spinster. "Evelina, my brother and I made this for your first baby." She handed her a beautiful woven blanket.

"I love it," said Evelina, taking it from her and running her fingers over the soft wool.

"Muriel and her brother, Isaac, once had their own shop and are skilled at spinning and weaving," Claude told her.

"I was the merchant's daughter," said Muriel, holding the hand of her three-year-old son, Glen. The rest of her four children ran around chasing Isobel's three boys as well as Claude's sister, Charlotte.

"Lord Nicholas married you, yet you weren't a noble?" she asked in astonishment.

"He did," said Muriel. "Sometimes love is stronger that status."

"I wanted to marry you even when I thought you were only a handmaid," Claude reminded Evelina.

"And I would have married you if you were naught but a commoner," Evelina told him in return.

Evelina's father cleared his throat. "So, Montague, where will you be living with my daughter? In England or France?"

"Yes, Claude," said John. "If you are ready to leave France behind, I have plenty of room for you and Evelina and any children you might have in my new castle. I would love to spend more time with you, Son."

"Where will we live, Claude?" asked Evelina, looking up in question.

Claude felt torn. Now that Evelina was his wife, her family resided in France. He was lord of Stonebury Castle in France, yet he wanted to spend more time getting to know his father in England. Plus, his mother and younger sister resided in England as well. A body of water separated his family.

He looked up to the ruins of Castle Hastings, breathing in a deep breath of fresh, sea air. Even from the ashes, one can rise again, he realized. There was no need to choose between his past and future because he could have it all living in the present.

"We will live in both places," he told Evelina.

"How can we do that?" she wondered.

"We will spend most of our time in France, but several months out of the year we will live in Winchelsea with my parents and sister."

"Oh, I would like that," said Claude's mother, always wanting to be close to him.

"That's a wise choice, Son," said John. "I am looking forward to it."

Claude's squire, Felix, ran over and interrupted the conversation. "Lady Rose is still feeling weak and can't leave the wagon. She wants to congratulate both of you. So does Lord Toft."

"Aye, I'd like to see the baby again," said Evelina, holding on to the blanket and taking Claude's hand as they strolled over to the wagon to talk to Rose and Toft.

"I am very happy for you," said Rose, sitting in the wagon, holding her baby to her chest. The baby started to cry. Toft took it from her, making silly faces and noises, trying to make it stop fussing.

"How are you feeling?" asked Evelina.

"I am still weak, but I will be fine thanks to both of you. So will Daniela. I can't thank you enough for being my friends."

"We'll always be your friends." Claude reached up and hugged Rose and kissed her on the cheek.

"Claude, you are married now and shouldn't be kissing other women," Rose told him.

"It's all right," said Evelina. "Claude and I know that our love is real and nothing can come between us."

"That's right," said Claude, gathering Evelina into his arms and kissing her passionately. "I hope to start raising a family soon because I can't wait to be a father." He dipped Evelina and bent over and kissed her again. She laughed as they both ended up falling on the ground.

"Save that for the bedchamber, Son," John called out. "After all, you need to learn what you can and cannot do in public."

"Nay, Father, you are wrong," Claude called back with a huge smile on his face. He looked deeply into Evelina's eyes when he said the next words. "With our love, there are no bounds, and nothing at all is **Forbidden**."

FROM THE AUTHOR

I hope you enjoyed Claude's story, as he finally now has his happily-ever-after with Evelina. If you would like to leave a review for me, it would be appreciated.

Most marriages of the medieval times were solely for purposes of alliances. However, it wouldn't be a romance if

FROM THE AUTHOR

I couldn't tweak situations to make them more romantic and the way we would like to see them.

Writing this story wasn't that easy because of the fact Claude was still in love with Rose from many years earlier. When we first met him, he was just a scrawny boy with long hair and his own father, who didn't know him, thought he was a girl. Claude has come a long way since then and shows his heroic side and love for Evelina when he steps up to the plate and faces off against her betrothed to protect her.

If you would like to read the story where Claude is first introduced in the series, you will want to pick up **The Baron's Destiny – Book 3** of the **Barons of the Cinque Ports Series**. You will also find the backstory of Claude's parents and their romance and the trials and troubles they went through, including the devastation of John losing his castle in the end. That book was inspired by a real-life event back in the late 1200s. A horrible storm came through and silted-up the harbor of Hastings which was one of the biggest ports of trade at the time. Hastings Castle really did break off with part of it falling into the sea.

The other books of the Cinque Ports series that have the stories of Lord Nicholas Vaughn and Lord Conlin de Braose are **The Baron's Quest – Book 1**, and **The Baron's Bounty – Book 2**.

Since a lot of my readers have been asking to know

about the families of my main characters after the books end, I am adding a list of the three barons and their families long after their stories end. The ages of their children are at the time of the book, **Forbidden**.

From *The Baron's Quest*:

Baron Nicholas Vaughn – Lord of New Romney

Muriel Draper – his wife (Once a spinster – spun wool, has brother, Isaac)

Their children: Twins, Nicholas and Nelda 8, Holly – 7, Heather – 5, Glen – 3

From *The Baron's Bounty*:

Baron Conlin de Braose – Lord of Sandwich (lost wife and 5 children through the years)

Isobel MacEwen – Conlin's wife. (Scottish - Once a proxy for her cousin, Catherine)

Their children: Rose - 21 (from Conlin's first marriage)

Torrence – 8, Dunmor – 6, Harry – 4

Rose and Sir Toft (Once Conlin's squire) married with baby Daniela (Lost 2 babies)

From *The Baron's Destiny*:

Baron John Montague – Lord of Hastings

Celestine de Bar – his French wife

Their children: Claude Jean – 23, Charlotte – 8

Watch for more stories of secondary characters from any of my series in my **Second in Command Series. Pirate in the**

FROM THE AUTHOR

Mist – Book 1, is the story of Rowen the Restless' first mate from the ***Legendary Bastards of the Crown Series.***

Remember, that to find your future happiness, you need to stop living in the past and concentrate on the precious present.

Elizabeth Rose

ABOUT ELIZABETH

Elizabeth Rose is a multi-published, bestselling author, writing medieval, historical, contemporary, paranormal, and western romance. She is an amazon all-star and has been an award finalist numerous times. Her books are available as Ebooks, paperback, and audiobooks as well.

Her favorite characters in her works include dark, dangerous and tortured heroes, and feisty, independent heroines who know how to wield a sword. She loves writing 14th century medieval novels, and is well-known for her many series.

Her twelve-book small town contemporary series, Tarnished Saints, was inspired by incidents in her own life.

After being traditionally published, she started self-publishing, creating her own covers and book-trailers on a dare from her two sons.

Elizabeth loves the outdoors. In the summertime, you can find her in her secret garden with her laptop, swinging in her hammock working on her next book. Elizabeth is a born storyteller and passionate about sharing her works with her readers.

Please be sure to visit her website at **Elizabethrosenovels.com** to read excerpts from any of her novels and get sneak peeks at covers of upcoming books. You can follow her on **Twitter, Facebook, Goodreads** or **Bookbub.**

Be sure to sign up for Elizabeth Rose's Readers' Group and also her newsletter, so you don't miss out on new releases or upcoming events.

ALSO BY ELIZABETH ROSE

Medieval

Legendary Bastards of the Crown Series
Season of Fortitude Series
Legacy of the Blade Series
Daughters of the Dagger Series
MadMan MacKeefe Series
Barons of the Cinque Ports Series
Second in Command Series

Medieval/Paranormal

Elemental Series
Greek Myth Fantasy Series
Tangled Tales Series

Contemporary

Tarnished Saints Series

Western

Cowboys of the Old West Series

Please visit http://elizabethrosenovels.com

Elizabeth Rose

Made in the USA
Columbia, SC
26 June 2018